D1524071

Erasing Secrets

The Lyons Garden Book Two

D.M. Foley

Independently Published

This book is dedicated to the readers. Without you, I am not an author. I am merely a writer of words. With you, my words come alive. Your support of my dream means the world to me and I thank you all from the very bottom of my heart. I hope you continue to enjoy my creativity.

"Believe me, every heart has its secret sorrows, which the world knows not, and oftentimes we call a man cold, when he is only sad"
HENRY WADSWORTH LONGFELLOW

Contents

Chapter 1: Winter Chill

Winter on Gardiners Island started early, with the first snow falling in the first week of December. It began as a light snowfall to cover the ground and the treetops. The soft sea breeze carried the fluffy snow into little drifts here and there, mimicking the dunes along the beach.

Bundled up, Jimmy rode his ATV around the island, doing his security rounds. Occasionally stopping to drink from the thermos full of hot coffee Stella had made for him. The coffee did wonders, warming him from the inside out.

It had been weeks since Mary had committed suicide, and someone had pushed Alexandria to her death. The hush of the snowfall amplified the quiet stillness that had encompassed the island since those tragic events had unfolded.

He had no evidence that Mary hadn't actually committed suicide. The investigating he had done refuted that she was the one that almost drowned Jessica. So Mary's confession to that act still did not ring faithful to him. This made him question her apparent suicide.

None of it proved out. No rationale why Mary would confess crimes she could not have committed. However, his daily remorse over her suicide was a completely different story. His disdain for her past transgressions had led her to make the very permanent, rash decision to end her life. She was his biological mother. That truth had been the ultimate shock.

Jimmy had known Ms. Mary his entire life. The adoptive son of Stella and John Driscoll, growing up on the island as he walked through the Manor house gardens with the woman he knew as Ms. Mary. His parents worked on the island while he spent time with her. She had loved him even when she didn't know he was indeed her son. The grief she felt being forced to give up her child ironically healed by the very child she had given birth to. Without the understanding, the child was hers.

After making his morning rounds, he wound up at the family cemetery. Jimmy placed a small bouquet on Mary's grave after wiping the accumulation of snow off her headstone. It was her birthday. Compelled to pay his respects to the woman that had given him life. He let a single tear roll down his cheek.

The eerie silence with snow falling, compounded by realizing the tragic losses the cemetery had held, sent a shiver up his spine. Then, turning to leave, noticing a new memorial box lovingly left recently at Alexandria's headstone. Jimmy smiled, knowing that it was Arthur who had put it there. Arthur visited Alexandria weekly and did a great job honoring her by taking care of her plot and headstone.

Jimmy had noticed the change in Arthur

since Alexandria's death. His usual cheerful demeanor had turned glum and depressive. His conversations were short and sweet. They mostly filled those talks with business issues or legal issues that needed to be handled. Jimmy tried to help by inviting him to the family Thanksgiving he had hosted. However, Arthur didn't feel very festive and had declined the invite.

The hope that Christmas would be different, Jimmy had already extended the invitation for Arthur to join the family for the holiday coming up. Arthur said he would think about it. Jimmy had already bought gifts for the family, making trips to the mainland. The presents piled up fast from him.

He had found some pretty cool filters and lenses for Jessica. He knew she would enjoy using them in her photography. It still amazed him they shared a birthday, and they were cousins. Neither of them had known their biological families until a few months ago. It had been a whirlwind discovery that had thrown them into the throes of owning and running the island and a multimillion-dollar real estate company.

His life on the island hadn't changed too much. Other than moving from his parent's small farmhouse to the Manor house on the island. He had stayed the head of security. The only difference was the weekly trip into the city to sit on the real estate business board meeting.

That aspect of the additional responsibilities was demanding. In keeping Jimmy's secret and the reasons for him being there were wearisome. Lies told to the inhabitants, and even the board members, were burdensome.

Thankful for his Uncle Richard. Who had more business prowess and understanding than Jimmy or Jessica would ever have. It made managing the business easier for them both.

Jessica had expressed to him frequently that she was also thankful that her father was savvy with the company. It gave her the freedom to continue doing her photography business.

Jimmy knew planning her wedding with Timothy took up a lot of Jessica's time. They had picked the date of July seventh to be wed on the island in the Manor house garden at the gazebo. It thrilled her parents that they had made that decision and they were excitedly helping with the plans. Jimmy, though, was apprehensive. The information he knew about Mary's death and confession weighed heavily on his mind and worried him.

The knowledge of the small wedding party eased his mind slightly. Jessica had asked her sister Samantha to be her maid of honor. Timothy was still searching for any trace of his biological family. Sadly, despite having a second cousin match on the genealogy website, there had been no response to his inquiry. Unfortunately, Timothy had no brothers through his adoptive parents. Compounded by him not having any close male friends. So Timothy asked her brother Richard to be his best man. Being adopted and having no siblings, Jimmy could relate and sympathize with Timothy's plight.

Jimmy found it sad Timothy's adoptive parents were angry with him for attempting to find out who his biological parents were and had disowned him. Even the news of him meeting Jessica and asking her to marry him hadn't softened their hearts to their perceived betrayal by him. Timothy had expressed feeling blessed over meeting Jessica when he did. Their relationship had started only a few months prior and had blossomed quickly. Feeling graced with the supportive and loving adoptive parents, Jimmy empathized with Timothy.

Timothy and Jimmy had quickly become good friends after their rocky start. They could laugh now at the fact Jimmy thought Timothy was the one behind Jessica's near-drowning and ATV accident. Those events that occurred were perplexing to them all. The peculiar way they had brought together the family was a silver lining to the chaos.

Walking into the Manor kitchen to grab some breakfast from Stella, Jimmy continued contemplating the last few months of his life.

"Morning, my son. You look down on this beautiful day."

"Thinking about the last few months. The craziness of it all. Feeling blessed for you and Dad, but also feeling sad about Ms. Mary."

"Ah, I know your life has changed, and I know you must still grieve the loss of Ms. Mary, your mother, but she would want you to move on, son."

"I know, Ma, it's just hard. I feel guilty, you know. If I hadn't had such a powerful reaction, she wouldn't have killed herself."

"Son, it wasn't your fault. You reacted the way anyone would have in your shoes. She reacted the way she felt was right for her. Ms. Mary

always only thought of herself and how things affected her. It was her biggest fault and was her downfall."

"I know all of that, but it doesn't change the way I feel."

"It's okay to feel a little guilty, and it means you are human and you care. I would worry if you didn't feel a bit of guilt. However, don't live there in guilt. Feel it, acknowledge it, forgive yourself, and move on from it."

"Thanks, Mom. I love you. Please never change. Remember, you and Dad will always be my number one parents. No matter what. I know I am feeling the loss of my mother, but I am thankful for you."

Jimmy finished his breakfast and headed back out into the swirling snow.

Samuel, the mechanic, passed by Jimmy as he climbed back onto his ATV.

"Morning, Jimmy."

"Good morning, Samuel. It's a cold one today."

"Yup."

"Stay warm. Stella's got coffee brewing in the kitchen. You can help yourself to some."

"Thanks, maybe I will. Later."

"You are welcome. Have a good day."

"You too."

Jimmy could tell he was busy fixing something because grease covered his overalls. Samuel, a quiet man, could restore any machine on the island. This made him a valuable asset to the island's operations. An employee for the last 22 years. With no family ties to the place. Most had grown up on the island their entire lives, like Jimmy.

As he watched, Samuel climbed into his pickup truck and headed toward the ferry to the mainland. Jimmy figured he was on the hunt to get some parts. This was a common occurrence.

At the security shack, Jimmy met up with a few of his security crew.

Zach was a 20-year-old who had

joined the security team when he graduated from high school. His father, Matt, was also a member of the crew. They were both sitting, monitoring the radio chatter of the rest of the team. Four team members were out on two boats patrolling the island perimeter from the water. Four other members were out on ATVs roaming the vast acres of the island. Today, with the snow falling and the wind blowing, it wasn't a fun job.

Most days, though, they all found their job to be exciting. They routinely caught teenagers coming ashore by boat to party on the beaches on the island. After reading about Captain Kidd burying his glory on the island, some searched for pirate treasure. Then the regular tabloid journalists always dogged the family.

Since Richard's mysterious return to the island after Alexandria's death, and Mary's suicide, the tabloid journalists had been more frequent. The change in the weather should curb the influx, though. Most journalists seemed to be fair-weather friends, so Jimmy and his crew looked forward to a much-needed reprieve.

"*Hey, boss. When is the Gardiner family coming out for the holidays?*" Zach asked.

"*A few days before Christmas Eve,*" Jimmy said.

He raised his eyebrows.

Zach was usually shy and rarely asked questions about the comings and goings of anyone on the island. Jimmy was curious why now he seemed interested in the family's arrival.

"*ALL of them are coming, right? Even Samantha,*" Zach said.

He was smiling from ear to ear.

There it was. Zach had a crush on Samantha. Jimmy laughed and patted him on the back. Jimmy was a sucker for immature love.

"*Yes, Samantha will be here. Do you want me to introduce you to her?*"

Zach got extremely quiet, blushing, and shook his head yes.

"Get spruced up for the party. I will definitely introduce you to her."

"Sounds like a plan, boss. Now don't forget."

"How could I forget to introduce two potential love birds?"

The plan was to introduce them during the Christmas Eve open house. He was planning on hosting it for the island inhabitants and the family. Matt, Zach's father, just chuckled and shook his head at the two men's exchange. Secretly, he was hoping his son would hit it off with the younger Gardiner daughter. Relation to the family through marriage wouldn't be a bad thing.

"Hey Zach, if you play your cards right, you may end up part-owner of the island."

"Dad, don't rush things. Samantha is a mainlander and you know how they can be towards us."

"Don't sell yourself short, son. You have what it takes to win her heart."

"Ah. I hope so. I don't want to be a part-

owner. That is just way too much responsibility. I want to know the green-eyed beauty with red flowing hair."

Matt chuckled again. He had grown up on the island. Both his parents grew up there, got married, and raised their family. He was the only one that stayed and had gotten a job himself on the island, raising his own family. His wife helped take care of the gardens.

Many older families like him found it harder and harder to convince their children to stay and continue living there. He was happy Zach enjoyed working for the security team alongside him. His college daughter had no aspiration to come back. Few jobs available made living on the mainland more appealing to the younger generations.

"Don't run off with the mainlander and leave your parents."

"Why would I leave here? I have the best job!"

The biggest job was security. The wives of the security team worked the sprawling gardens around the Manor house. There were a few specialty jobs. Stella was the Manor house cook, Martin the butler, and Betty, the housekeeper. Captain Bill, the ferry captain, had a small crew that helped him run the ferry to and from the island. Of course there was also, Samuel, the mechanic.

Jimmy knew losing the family atmosphere on the island was inevitable. How soon that occurred was the question. For now, he was thankful that he had Zach and Matt.

"This party will be different."

"I am excited to take part in festivities instead of being outsiders, looking in."

"I am glad you are excited. I hope others are as well."

"Oh, others definitely are! It is the talk of the island! You are doing good, Jimmy. I am proud of you."

Matt was hoping for a change on the island. Maybe that would bring his daughter back. He hoped she would hear of the changes and give it a shot. The thought of his family's legacy on the island eventually dying out saddened him.

"*I am making it a family atmosphere. Instead of us vs. them. The younger family members are unique. Maybe since they didn't grow up knowing they were part of the Gardiner family.*"

"*I hope so, boss. I want to know them better. Especially, Samantha.*"

"*I think you are going to like them all, Zach. Not just Samantha.*"

"*Well, I am only interested in her. I am sure they're all nice.*"

"*You realize being friends with her brothers will be a benefit to you, right?*"

"*Yeah, I am aware. I need to know her first. She may not even like me. No sense wasting time befriending her brothers.*"

"*You have a point there. Don't forget, she has a big sister too. And from what I have learned about her, she is feisty.*"

"*Honestly, I am not worried about the big sis-*

ter. I am used to big sisters. They don't scare me."

Jimmy just shook his head at Zach. Not wanting to think about change or Zach's sister. The change would come, though. It was inevitable.

They would have to replace people when they retired with others from the mainland. Something he didn't want to do. He knew bringing more mainlanders onto the island would eventually taint the entire island. Ultimately wanting to usher in mainland ideas to the tranquility of the island. Samuel mentioned to Jimmy the island would make a great tourist resort occasionally.

While he understood Samuel's idea, he knew Samuel didn't understand the love of the island most of the inhabitants had. It was history. It was untouched by the outside world. In places on the island, one could feel transported. Native Americans had lived there. They could feel the spirits of the generations of ancestors from the past. Jimmy found many arrowheads and other artifacts over the years. He couldn't imagine desecrating the island with a resort.

Jimmy left the security shack and started his afternoon rounds. He noticed the snow had stopped falling. They had received about three inches of accumulation throughout the morning. He could hear the roar of a truck engine coming up the road. Jimmy recognized it as Samuel's.

When Samuel got out of his truck, he headed towards the cemetery instead of the garage. Jimmy noticed the bouquet in Samuel's hands. He watched from a distance as Samuel placed the spray of white roses at Mary's grave. It was touching to watch someone else pay their respects on her birthday.

It made sense Samuel would, considering Mary had hired him. Moreover, she left him a sizable chunk of her estate so that he might have felt a sense of obligation towards her. Whatever the reason, it warmed his heart that someone else remembered his biological mother's birthday.

Chapter 2: Secrets

The most minute detail could spoil the best-laid plans. An early snowstorm was a stark reminder of that. The layer of snow would make it hard not to leave a trace. They had done well until now, hiding their comings and goings.

In a few short weeks, the family would return. However, plans formed made them feel that revenge would bring them elation.

The cage of crows crowded the back bedroom. Their cawing had become loud and annoying, so they threw a sheet over the cage to quiet the noise. But, smiling, they couldn't wait till they could silence the lot of them for good. In due time, the blasted birds would serve their purpose.

As they sat thinking about the crows, a childhood memory crept into their mind. They had been out on a walk. They had found a fledgling that had fallen out of its nest and could not find the nest. It had proven fruitless. They brought the fledgling home and put it in a shoebox.

Mom had become irate in a drunken stupor, yelling, why did they carry another mouth in the house to feed? She provided little for them as it was. Her gentleman caller had taken the shoebox. They remembered how he grabbed the fledgling with aggression from the box and snapped its neck. Right there, in front of them all.

This hadn't horrified them. Instead, the finality and swiftness of it all fascinated them.

One minute the fledgling was alive, and the next, it was lying limp with its head hanging. The power that this man had displayed lit them on fire. Did they hold the same power? To control another living being's life and subsequent death?

As they sat contemplating that thought, a cockroach crawled from behind the couch. They had grabbed it, held it between their fingers, and twisted it. They had kept rotating until the creature was in two parts. This act ignited a sense of life they hadn't felt before.

Until that point, they had just existed for 10 yrs. Not living, just surviving. School was boring, and they had no real friends. Not even the other children on the island. They now felt a purpose, though. They could choose what lived or died or who.

That memory made them smile. They came far since that day. With each kill, they felt stronger. When they took each creature's life, something transferred its essence to them. The power they expected to feel in the future excited them. They needed patience for it all to work out.

The snow posed a problem. They had to spy on the family without being caught. Jimmy locking the door to the attic took some wind out of their sails. They used those passage-ways for years, spying on the inhabitants. They knew all the family secrets, good and bad.

Their mother was one of the dirty little secrets. One day, following her, is how they had found the passageways. Mom got dolled up. She said she was going out. When she wound up at the Manor house going through the passageways and ending up in the Lord of the Manor's bed. Their first glimpse of the darkness.

Mother's purpose, servicing the Lord with the Lady away. In return, she could live in one of the servant's homes on the island with her child. They gave her a day job to obscure her actual occupation.

They were six and didn't quite understand what the two naked adults were doing. Curiosity engulfed them, they became interested in the physical interactions between the two.

There wasn't love, at least not from him. Mother kissed this man differently than the others. It was clear she cared more about him. Clear even to a young child. The man was dismissive towards her.

On his part it was pure desire, though.

Both participants registered pleasure, although it seemed almost abusive with the intensity they both displayed.

From that night forward. The passageways themselves were used to gather all the secrets they could. There were plenty with the Gardiner family. The outside world thought the family had perfect lives. They came to know the brutal truth.

As a child, they didn't quite understand the power these secrets wielded. The older they got. The more they appreciated the potential the secrets held.

Many times. A phone call to the tabloids would have ruined the family in its entirety. They didn't, though. Instead, they gathered and documented everything they could and kept the secrets hidden from everyone. The unknown, known to them, and holding the key to a whole family's destiny, felt powerful. The power they craved and lived for. Energy they killed for and would again.

The family had done an excellent job itself of unearthing several secrets. Richard, coming out of hiding, had been a big one. They hadn't seen that one coming. One secret they hadn't known. The entire world had thought he died in the tragic sailboat accident. Instead, surviving, and started a new life with his mistress of several years. That life was happy until Alexandria's death.

Much as her death had given them such a sense of power and purpose, it was incidental. Not planned, at least not so soon. They had tried to start a discussion with the old bat. Tried to reveal one secret they knew to be the truth. She hadn't wanted to listen, even when they tried showing her proof. They had tried to grab her to stop her from walking away and had made her lose her balance. She had fallen down the stairs in a crumpled mess. Surprised, she survived for a few days. She had told police someone pushed her. However, she hadn't said by whom. That was the most bewildering part. She had known. That is one secret she kept till her death.

Her death had become a catalyst for so many unearthed secrets. How Mary's betrayal of Richard's trust had revealed the truth about their lost child. That child, who was not Richard's, was also a Gardiner descendant. Just another of the dark secrets. Very few knew about Jimmy. Only the Gardiner family themselves, Arthur and Jimmy's adoptive parents, and them. Knowing this brought a flutter to their heart and a gleam to their eyes.

That secret would be useful. When the time came. It would come. Secrets were powerful weapons used at the right time. They could serve them well. Mary's secrets had benefited them well a few months ago. They had gotten the police off the island.

The police presence had made them paranoid. They hadn't expected the authorities to become involved, even with the accidents that had occurred. All explainable as accidents. The old bat told police someone pushed her down the stairs. That's when things changed. They devised a plan to get the police off the island. It could have been bad if they had stayed and investigated longer.

However, Richard returning and causing

the chaos of unearthed secrets had set up a perfect scenario to remove the police. Mary's reaction was predictable, which helped them get rid of her. That night had worked out. Mary had locked herself in her room and started drinking, which was her standard practice when upset.

They had seized on the opportunity and snuck through the passageway. Mary set up the bathwater, as they watched, giving them the perfect setup to stage her suicide. They had added a few pills to the wine glass when they distracted Mary with the cell phone calls. Then waited until she was incoherent to be coached to write the note. They had added the rest of the pills to her last glass of wine and watched as she drifted into unconsciousness.

As Mary slipped under the water, they

remembered watching the bubbles from her nose and mouth end. She served her purpose well. They smiled again at the thought of every secret serving a purpose.

Lunch break was over. They had to get back to work. The mundane chore of their everyday existence bored them. They needed to release some pent-up frustration, needed a power rush before returning to work, and needed to feel alive.

The covered cage of crows was tempting. They thought about just taking one. Would it matter if they killed one earlier than planned? Could the remains serve a purpose if it was decomposing already?

Out of the corner of their eye, they saw a field mouse scurry across the counter. They mused at the perfect timing. With swift experience, they caught the mouse and hung onto its tail. The mouse struggled to get out of the grip of their fingers.

Slow and calculated. Fast and furious. Those choices they had to make. Each had its pros and cons. Each also had its satisfying reward. They went slow and calculated and filled the kitchen sink with water.

They lowered headfirst the mouse into the water; they pulled it out just as it slowed its struggle. Then, as it caught its breath and wriggled to life again, they lowered it again into the water. They repeated the process until the mouse no longer regained its breath and was lifeless in their fingers.

They tossed the dead mouse into the trash, sighing. They washed up, put their coat on, and headed back to work, feeling alive with energy. The rush never got old. The small kills didn't give a big lift or energy boost as the big kills, though.

They needed a hunt for a more significant kill. Later, seeing if they could get a kill out in the fields. One to hold them for longer. They needed to hold out a few more weeks.

To plan was crucial, anticipating snow a few days earlier. They had ordered a drone to assist them in spying on the family. It came quickly. It would help them gather more secrets. The more secrets they had, the more power they held.

They had plenty of time to learn how to use it. Maybe they would take it hunting with them later. That solved the problem of leaving tracks in the snow while spying outside. Then they had the brilliant idea of bugging rooms in the Manor house. Technology was becoming their best friend.

The rest of the afternoon was routine. They went about their work as normal, seeing Jimmy doing his rounds on his ATV. They watched and pondered how he would react when his secrets came out. He wouldn't be able to deny them. There was too much proof. His secrets would play a vital role in their plans for the family.

With the darkness, they would erase every family secret, except one.

Chapter 3: Family Tensions

Jessica was watching the snowfall out her window as she drank her cup of tea. They called the board meeting off because of the impending storm. She found herself with nothing planned for the day. Timothy was away for the next week on an assignment. Jessica was lonely. This would have been their first snowstorm together.

She seized on having nothing planned and looked at wedding dresses online. There were only eight months until she and Timothy would say their nuptials. She wanted nothing too frilly or too girly-girl. Not too long or too short. Dresses were not her forte. The thought of all eyes on her while wearing one terrified her.

The wedding would be outside, in the gazebo of the Manor house in July. Comfort was her principal goal, with a splash of elegance and primary simplicity being her prominent style. Her mother, Mira, wanted her to wear grace and frills, more of a princess-type gown.

The thought annoyed Jessica. She wasn't good at pretending to be something she wasn't. Elegant was not a quality anyone knew Jessica to be. The thought was downright laughable. When she drank with guys she hung around with, she drank them under the table. She belched with the best of them, and downed shots like there was no tomorrow.

This difference in styles and personality traits had added some tension to the whole wedding planning with her mother. Especially after Jessica's parents presented her to her biological grandparents, Brad and Kathleen Kennedy. They were the epitome of materialistic snobs.

They had gushed over finding Jessica, apologizing for having Mira give her up for adoption, yet claiming it all had worked out for the best in the end. The shock for them was learning the truth about Mira and Richard's relationship and that Richard was Jessica's father. Their anger subsided. The realization came. It related them through marriage to a wealthy and influential family, the Gardiners.

The more Jessica got to know them, the more she despised them. This made her feel guilty since they were family, after all. She just couldn't understand their materialism. Every week, her grandmother would call her up and invite her to go clothes shopping with her mother and sister.

When she went the first time, she couldn't believe the number of clothes they all bought compared to what she wound up buying. She needed a couple of new pairs of jeans and a few sweaters. That was the difference, though. She needed what she had purchased, and the others just bought it because they wanted it.

She had visited her parent's home after that first shopping spree, and her sister had shown her a closet full of clothes with the tags still on them. This had dumbfounded Jessica. She couldn't fathom owning so many clothes, let alone not wearing half of what she owned.

Raised by the Greenhalls, Jessica had learned humbleness and thankfulness for everything. They had never gone without.

However, they didn't live with excess either. Instead, they had shown her how to live off the land. They gardened and grew most of their fruits and vegetables, canning and freezing to use throughout the year. Deer hunting was a big thing for them, filling their freezers every year with enough game to last until the next season.

The first time Jessica had her biological family to her house for dinner, she had cooked some venison steaks marinated in raspberry vinaigrette. They all ate it and commented on how delicious the meal had been. When they asked where she had gotten such flavorful steaks, though, horror-filled them finding out they had eaten deer meat that she had killed. Afterward, her grandmother had gone on a two-week vegetarian cleanse diet to purge her body of the *Bambi* meat, as she had put it.

Jessica chuckled to herself when she re-membered their horror. The wedding planning caused tension, and more than once, she sug-gested they take a trip to Vegas and elope. Tim-othy reminded her, though, they planned on getting married once, so they should do it the way they wanted. He figured out how to keep her calm and rational. One of the many reasons she had fallen in love with him. Thoughts of him now only made her miss him more.

Despite hoping to find her perfect dress online, she realized her search was futile. She had hoped to find one online to get out of shopping with her sister, mother, and grand-mother. Samantha set up an appointment at a dress shop in Boston. It would be a chance to look at bridal and bridesmaid dresses in person. She was nervous about shopping with the three of them present. However, she hoped to find the perfect dress.

Relaxation was necessary to ease the anxiety and tension she was feeling. Jessica bundled up, took one of her cameras, and went outside. Taking pictures of the falling snow, she loved catching the shimmer of sunlight reflected off the snowflakes. Along the edge of her yard, there was a row of cedar trees whose boughs and branches were bending with the weight of the falling snow. They created a brilliant winter wonderland tunnel.

Through the tunnel, walking, she got some pretty exceptional shots. Jessica loved to get different perspectives while taking pictures, so she laid down in the snow and took pictures of the snow tunnel from different angles. When she finished, she had gotten cold and decided it was time to go inside. As she shed her wet coat and snow pants, her cell phone rang. She smiled as she answered it.

"Hello, my love, I miss you."

"Ah, I miss you too. That is why I called. I needed to hear your voice."

"It's snowing here. You are missing our first snowfall. It's beautiful. I took a bunch of pictures just so I can show you."

"I can't wait to see the pictures, and I am sure they are not as beautiful as you."

"You always make me blush. How is the writing going?"

"I do my best to let you know how much I love you. I am lucky to have found you. The writing, it's going well. I am learning from the crocodile guides down here. Like, how not to get eaten

alive."

"I love you too and feel the same. Please take heed of what those guides tell you. I don't want to be a widow before we're married."

"I will be careful. Hey, speaking of the wedding. Do you think we could add crocodile stew to the menu? It's croco delicious!"

Jessica spit out the sip of tea she had just taken. She could just see the looks of alarm on her grandparent's faces if she mentioned crocodile stew was on the wedding menu.

"Hmm, maybe turtle soup as the appetizer?"

"Caterpillar crepes for dessert!"

Both of them burst into full belly laughter at their diabolical minds melding into one.

One thing was for sure. No matter what, they were decisive to have their wedding how they wished. They didn't care what anyone else thought. As they hung up the phone, Jessica felt better than she had felt earlier.

It still amazed her how much Timothy completed her life. She couldn't wait to be his wife. The thought of being the mother of his children also excited her. She knew the challenge of bringing up their children as she had been. Especially now that she had found her biological family and had inherited a million-dollar real estate company. Determination ran through her veins, though. She saw the differences between herself and her siblings, wanting her kids to be like her.

Timothy had expressed the same desire. He didn't like the materialism of her family. Their kids would work for what they needed and wanted in life. Even though his adoptive parents had disowned him for looking for his biological family, he was still grateful for his upbringing.

Jessica's heart ached for Timothy. She couldn't understand how his adoptive parents would disown him. Trying to help him find his biological family had become a priority for her. She wanted him to have family members at their wedding. They had few leads.

One second cousin matched on the genealogy website a few months prior. Timothy had messaged the person and had gotten no response. This perplexed her. Jessica logged onto the genealogy website and logged in to Timothy's account. She inspected the second cousin's tree. It was public, so she could try to disseminate information.

Going over the tree, a name jumped out at Jessica. Allison Simmons, could it be the same Allison that was the CEO of Cromwell Real Estate Investment Corporation? The same Allison that she sat across from at the board meetings? She wrote the tree information and would ask Allison more about herself and her family at their next meeting.

Was it a family connection for Timothy right under their noses? Nothing surprised her anymore after what she had been through finding her own family. She would keep the relationship a secret until she could verify or deny it. Not informing Timothy would be difficult. However, she wanted to spare him any potential disappointment.

Two days later, she was sitting in a meeting across from Allison. Discussing the latest project for the real estate company, an acquisition of an older building in Manhattan, and debating whether they wanted to demolish it and build brand new or renovate it.

"Can we get a cost analysis? What is the difference between the cost of renovating the existing building and demolishing it to build a new one?"

"Hmm, it might be a wise decision. I don't see why we can't."

It surprised Richard Jessica wanted the cost analysis.

However, she was leaning more towards the renovation because it was an older type of architecture. Her fondness for architecture made her appreciate the art in older buildings compared to the shiny tall buildings that marked the surrounding skyline. Maybe it was her photographic eye, or her affinity towards preserving history, that made her that way.

Allison was more inclined towards the demolition and rebuilding option.

"We have always demolished and built new in the past. It is better for resale value."

"I disagree, Allison. Having been to Dublin, I have seen how they blend old architecture with new."

In addition, her world travels had given her a different perspective than Allison. The latter had lived and worked in New York City her entire life.

"Well, you may have traveled the world, but I have worked in this city for years. I know what sells and what doesn't."

"That may be true, but we should look at all options and not just go with the status quo."

Richard, Jessica's father, was on the fence.

"You both have valid points. As a business,

we should concern ourselves with both costs of a project and the resale value."

He agreed with Allison about resale value. However, he listened to Jessica's arguments, which were impressive. He did not realize she knew about architecture. The desire for cost analysis of both options showed him she was learning this business fast.

Jimmy, being inclined to preserve history himself, was leaning towards Jessica's idea of remodeling the building. Willing to wait until they did the cost analysis to decide, though.

"I vote to do the cost analysis. It makes sense."

After the meeting, Jessica tried to strike up a casual conversation with Allison.

"Hey, Allison. I hope the board meeting didn't upset you? "

"No worries. Board meetings get heated. Debate is good for business."

"Oh Good. I realized the other day I know little about you. Even though we work with each other. So do you mind me asking you some questions? To get to know you better."

"Not at all. What do you want to know?"

Jessica, treading lightly and not getting too in-depth or personal. She wanted to know everything she could. She had to figure out how to ask her. So she went with the relatable approach.

"Well, I have three siblings I never knew I had. I am adjusting to having a big family coming from a small one. So, do you have siblings?"

"Yeah, I know your family story. That must be difficult to navigate. I have two older brothers, Thomas and Robert. We were close growing up.

However, now that we are older, we have our own lives."

"Oh, I am sorry. I didn't mean to bring up any bad feelings about your family."

"It's all good. My brothers are both married and have children. Me, I haven't found mister right yet. I am married to my work. And I have no children."

"Well, I hope you find your mister right. I feel blessed I met mine. I am grateful you're married to your work. This business needs you."

"I appreciate you saying that. Alexandria taught me well. I miss her, as I am sure everyone else does. She was like a mother to me."

Jessica smiled as she finished talking to Allison. She had gotten the confirmation she needed. It related Allison to the DNA match to Timothy in the family tree! Now to figure out if Allison and Timothy matched. Of course, she had to prove it, too. Could she even be his biological mother?

Chapter 4: Siblings

Samantha was excited about her sister's visit coming up on the weekend. The dress shop in Boston had to have the perfect bridal gown for Jessica. Although realizing her sister was being super picky. Confidence filled her. She would help Jessica find the right one and satisfy their mom's wishes.

She was getting ready for her Thursday night shift at the restaurant she waitressed at. Samantha braided her long, red hair. The servers had to wear black fitted skirts cut above their knees and a white top. Many of the girls she worked with hated the outfits for various reasons.

Not her though, she loved showing off her

long legs with the skirts. She knew men found her attractive, and she used that to her advantage. Flirting with the male customers had become an art form to her. Treading light when the men accompanied women, though.

It was never her intent to come between any couples. She wanted money to move out on her own. Not that she had to move. Her parents welcomed her to live at home as long as she wanted to. She just wanted some privacy. Being an adult and living at home had some downfalls.

The main pitfall was dating. Samantha's parents would give her the third degree over every guy she even mentioned or hung out with. A multitude of questions would berate the poor guys as well. These situations always led to awkwardness. So she flirted and got big tips, which she put in a jar in her closet.

She could ask her parents for the money to move out to be independent. They would give it to her. However, since meeting her big sister, she realized how privileged she had been. Determined to do this one thing on her own to prove she wasn't a spoiled rich brat.

Thursday nights were her favorite shift. Several regular customers would ask to be seated in her section. One guy about her own age was her favorite. A cheeseburger, fries, and soda were his regular meal. He was always so polite when he ordered, saying little besides placing his order, even when she turned on the charm. He smiled and laughed plenty at her flirtatious demeanor. It was rare that he bantered back. His tips were always good.

When she got to work, the restaurant was

already getting busy. She loved busy nights. Money filled her pockets on those evenings. She was skilled at providing exemplary customer service, quickly turning the tables over. If the kitchen kept up the pace, everything ran like clockwork for her.

Her regulars came, and the hostess seated them. She went up to each table and took their orders. When she came to her favorite regular, she smiled with a sparkle in her eye and a flip of her braid.

"What can I get you today, handsome?"

"I'll take the 8oz steak with a baked potato and the mac and cheese, please."

Zach blushed as he answered.

"Ah, changing it up, I see. How would you like that steak cooked?"

"Medium well, please."

"You got it! You want your usual drink, or are you changing that up too?"

"The usual, thank you."

"Anything for you, sweetie."

Samantha turned to walk away. Zach lifted his head up from looking at the menu. He blushed and smiled. Then, as his knees shook under the table. He got the courage up to reply.

"Anything? How about your number?"

His comeback surprised Samantha. He was so quiet and reserved. But she liked this new version. Of course, he still had his shyness, and she loved how she could make him blush. The quiet confidence he was getting, though, made him even more attractive than he already was. She turned back to him.

"I don't even know your name. You know my name, but I do not know yours."

"It's Zach."

"Well, Zach. It is nice to converse with you. But if I give you my number, you need to promise me you won't give it out or write it on the bathroom wall or anything."

"I promise, I would never do that."

"Okay, I will keep you to that promise. I look forward to talking with you more." Samantha handed him a slip of paper with her number on it.

He blushed again while taking the slip of paper from her fingertips. Their hands brushed, and she felt a jolt of electricity run through her. This time, she blushed.

At the end of her shift, she felt exhausted. She had done well with tips, and she put the thousand dollars into her jar at home. When she closed her eyes to go to bed, her thoughts went to Zach. She hoped he would call.

A first for her. She had never given her number to a customer. Plenty had asked. However, she either wasn't interested, or she just hadn't felt comfortable. It surprised her she was interested in him and felt secure with Zach.

Jessica arrived at her parent's house Friday evening. Their hugs comforted and their smiles genuine. Mira was excited about dress shopping the next day. The conversation at dinner revolved around the wedding plans. Jessica appreciated the excitement and the interest in helping. Although, she couldn't help feeling overwhelmed by her mother's insistence on certain things being done her way. It appeared it focused her mother more on the big wedding on the island that she and Richard could not have. This made it feel more about her mother and father. Rather than about her and Timothy.

The newness of their relationship made it hard for Jessica to stand up for herself and be assertive about her wishes. She didn't want to hurt her parent's feelings. Thankful for her brothers Richard Jr. and David changing the subject.

"Hey, Dad, David, and I have been doing some thinking."

"Yeah, we thought Jimmy could use some company in that big house on the island."

"I can work from anywhere, according to my employer. Plus, I could see Danielle more frequently."

"And I could help Jimmy bring the security on the island into the 21st century with cameras and *more technology."*

Jessica welcomed the reprieve from the wedding discussion. She thought her brother's idea was brilliant. Worry for Jimmy all alone in that big house had been on her mind. This would help ease her mind.

"What are your thoughts on this, Jessica?"

"I think it's a great idea! The boys could help share in the responsibility of watching over the island. But, of course, we would need to ask Jimmy his opinion too. He has a say in the matter."

"We can talk to Jimmy next week at our meeting. We will let you two know what he says."

Richard Jr. had fallen head over heels for Danielle. He just wanted to be closer. They had known each other their entire lives. Their moms were best friends from high school. Growing up, they had become best friends themselves. That friendship had grown. It blossomed into a romantic relationship, and they had dated the last few months.

Danielle had been there for him when his universe turned upside down. The shock of finding out he had an older sister. He hadn't known because his parents conceived her out of wedlock and because of an affair. Also, not knowing his sister because of the adoption. He learned his father had been leading a double life. Still married to his first wife and his mother. This knowledge had thrown him for a complete loop.

He felt graced he had Danielle helping through that tumultuous time. It was then he had realized he could no longer hold back his true feelings for her. They walked along the beach that night. He had told her about his family's secrets. Hand in hand. He had felt in seconds they were one.

The memories of that evening flooded his mind. When she halted, turning to face him, and wrapping her arms around him, hugging him. The tension in his body melted being held like that. That's when he had gotten the courage to kiss her. He had swept her long dark hair out of her brown eyes, leaned in, and kissed her soft lips.

She had tightened her hug and reciprocated the kiss with a little more fire than he had expected. He smiled, remembering how she had pulled away saying.

"It's about time you made that first move!"

They were a couple since. However, the long-distance relationship made it hard to see each other regularly. He was having thoughts of marriage and family with her. The distance, though, brought doubts into his mind about their relationship. This was why he wanted to move closer to her.

David just wanted a purpose. Fresh out of high school with no job. It was hard to figure out life. The knowledge of being a Gardiner had sparked an interest in his family history. He wanted to preserve that history and help protect the island and his family.

He had no desire to get involved in any relationships like his siblings. David wanted to have an established career first before getting involved with another person. Life was muddling enough. Without bringing another person's drama into it all.

It confused his inner feelings. Something attracted him to women. However, he felt he connected deeper with his male friends. He felt that soul connection. David didn't feel this with any female yet. This made him question his own sexuality. The soul connection excited him differently than his attraction to women. This was difficult for him to talk about to anyone.

He felt that living on the island with Jimmy and his brother Richard might help him untangle his own inner feelings. In addition, he knew his vast knowledge of computers and technology would help enhance security on the island. He hoped Jimmy would feel the same and welcome David and Richard onto the island.

The rest of the evening, discussions fluctuated between the wedding, the Christmas holiday coming up, the family business, and the boys moving to the island. Jessica felt a little inundated. She still was not used to the dynamics of a big family.

The tub called to her tired, tension-filled body. She drew the water, calling Timothy as she waited for it to fill the tub.

"Hey, beautiful. I am so glad you called. How is your visit home going?"

"It's going okay. I am just getting ready to take a tension-relieving bath."

"I wish I was there to massage that tension right out of you."

"Me too. Tonight, the bath will have to do."

Just hearing his voice soothed her soul. She shared the conversations of the evening with him. He agreed that Richard Jr.'s and David's plans to move to the island and the Manor house were great ideas.

They said their goodbyes, and she slipped into the tub to relax. She tried to close her eyes, yet the heart palpitations started, and she had to open them back up. The PTSD from almost being drowned made baths less relaxing. She couldn't talk to her family about it. They would not understand. Timothy was the sole person who knew about her PTSD.

The apparent quiet on the island since Mary's suicide eased her anxiety. This made it okay with her to be wed on the island.

Getting out of the tub and settling into bed, more relaxed. She dozed off, thinking about going dress shopping in the morning.

The sun was bright. It was the wedding day. Chairs formed rows with an aisle running down the center leading to the gazebo. Vines of clematis and roses entwined the gazebo. Something obscured the faces of the guests. At first, she thought it was because of her veil, then she realized she was lucid dreaming. It didn't feel right. Dark clouds came and covered the sun. Timothy was waiting at the gazebo for her. As she reached him, his hands outstretched towards her. Thunder boomed and lightning flashed. No, it wasn't thunder. It was gunshots. The smell of sulfur burned her nose, looking down and seeing the gun in her hand. Timothy lying at her feet in a puddle of blood. Her hands shaking, she dropped the gun and fell to her knees.

Jessica bolted up in her bed. Thank god it was just a nightmare! It had been years since she had a bad dream. This was upsetting. She dwelled on the meaning as she rested her head back on her pillow. She loved Timothy with her entire being. Why would her subconscious have her kill him? Jessica wanted to hold Timothy. She trembled at the fear of what the dream meant.

The last time she had a lucid dream, she had lost her adoptive father in a horrific car crash. She had the knowledge he passed before she even received the phone call. Was this an omen Timothy would die?

Praying. She asked God to please not take him from her.

Chapter 5: New & Old Love

It was Saturday, Jimmy's day off. However, Jimmy was so used to his daily routine that he rode his ATV around the island, even on his days off.

In addition, the snow from earlier in the week had melted, leaving mud everywhere he rode. So, since it was his day off, he had a bit of fun riding through the mud pits he encountered.

Off one of the beaten paths, he headed towards Willow Brook. He drove across and headed towards the two lookout towers on the island's eastern side. In the winter months, the woods were less dense, making it easier to ride through them with the ATVs.

He paused as he came across a deer carcass lying in his way. It was rare to find any wildlife dead around the island. Especially deer, since there were very few natural predators on the island. Those who hunted on the island hunted for food, not sport, and would never leave a carcass to rot.

He realized it was a few days old as he approached the carcass. The putrid stench was the first giveaway. Flies and maggots crawling all over the body were the next telltale sign. He covered his mouth and nose with the scarf he had around his neck. This gave him a bit of relief from the stench.

It was a decent-sized buck, at least an 8 pointer. There didn't seem to be a gunshot wound or an arrow wound. Upon closer inspection, Jimmy realized the gruesome truth.

This deer had its throat slit and its heart re-moved. *Who would do such a thing?* He thought to himself.

He used his radio to call for a security team to come and bury the poor animal. Then, taking out his phone, he took pictures of the scene.

There were no visible signs of anyone being around the carcass other than his foot-prints. However, he knew very well that the perpetrator could have snuck onto the island despite their best security efforts.

No one on the island would have done this in his mind. They were all connected too much to the land, and even though few had ties to the Native American ancestry of the island, they still respected it. This was a violation.

Zach and Matt showed up from the security team to help dispose of the deer. What they saw was shocking to them. Matt stepped closer.

"Who do you think did this, Jimmy?"

"Don't know. It makes no sense. No one on the island would do such a thing."

Zach stepped forward to get a better look.

"What a waste of a magnificent deer! That would have provided a couple of months' worth of meat."

"Exactly! That's why it makes no sense. Someone from the outside must have somehow got on the island. Maybe they took the heart like some sort of sick souvenir."

The men dug a hole and buried the deer. They were somber as they worked. Growing up on the island, they all respected the wildlife that lived alongside them. This was a stark reminder that some did not have that same respect.

It was also a crisp nudge that their security wasn't foolproof. The security team was going to have to step it up a bit to ensure the safety of the wildlife. In addition, security rounds would have to be expanded to include more of the secluded interior aspects of the island. The thought gave Jimmy an instant headache.

They were already a skeleton crew regarding the size of the island. There were few people left they could hire as added security. This was going to be a logistical nightmare for him. He hopped back on his ATV and continued his ride.

He hoped it would clear his head a bit. Thoughts went to the deer. He wondered if he should mention it to Jessica and Richard at this week's meeting. Things had been so quiet, he really didn't want to bring up the memories of the past couple of months.

At this moment, he really didn't think there was any connection between the past incidents and this one. Deciding to keep this under wraps for now, he drove back to the security shack to come up with some tentative plans for increased security.

Zach and Matt were both back at the shack. It was their lunch break. However, neither was all that hungry after dealing with the deer carcass. So instead, Matt read the local paper, trying to erase the images from his mind. While Zach focused on his phone.

They both looked up as Jimmy entered the building. Zach and Matt shook their heads. They knew he was not visiting on his day off.

The guy was a workaholic, and everyone knew it.

Jimmy noticed Zach had stopped typing on his phone.

"Don't let me interrupt your lunch break conversation. I just need to work out some logistics regarding upping security around here."

"Do you need any help, boss? You shouldn't be doing all this on your day off."

"I appreciate your offer, Zach. Enjoy your lunch break. I haven't seen you smile like that, ever. So whoever you are texting is clearly more important, especially after this morning. You deserve the escape."

Zach blushed.

"It's Samantha Gardiner. I have been going up to Boston to eat at the restaurant where she works for weeks now. Thursday nights, since I

have Thursday and Friday off. I finally got the courage to ask her for her number. We have been texting on and off since. So, I guess you don't have to introduce us at Christmas."

"My man, good for you! Just don't hurt her. You know she has siblings. Not to mention, it's literally my job to protect her."

Jimmy patted Zach on the back.

"I have no intentions of hurting her! You forget it's literally my job also to protect the Gardiners."

Zach was smiling from ear to ear.

Zach's happiness meant the world to Jimmy. They were like brothers, both growing up on the island. They went to school together on the mainland. Their fathers both worked for the security team. The differences in their lives were Zach had a sister, Jimmy had no siblings, and Jimmy was 5 years older. But he had no doubts that Zach would be good to Samantha.

Thoughts about Zach and Samantha got him thinking about his own love life. It was pretty nonexistent. When Zach's sister Melissa moved away to college, his hopes of love and marriage shattered. They had dated throughout high school. Both being from the island made it hard for them to fit in with the mainland kids.

They had grown up together. Jimmy and Melissa weren't always friends, though. As kids playing after school, he recalled they were often outright mean to one another. Sometimes pushing each other into Willow Brook or even putting frogs down each other's pants. She had been more of a tomboy back then,

Till puberty hit them both. That's when Jimmy and Melissa both noticed each other in a peculiar light. Freshman year, they had dated, and they stayed a couple till graduation day. That's when she broke up with him and told him she was leaving for college in the fall. When she told him she had no plans to return to the island, it devastated him.

She had kept her word, too. In the seven years after leaving, she hadn't come back. Not once. Her family visited her once or twice a year in upstate New York.

Jimmy had tried to move on. He dated a few women here and there from the mainland. But, unfortunately, his mind always wandered to Melissa. He compared every woman to his lost love. No matter what, he could not get her out of his mind.

For now, he was content with his bachelor's lifestyle. He enjoyed living by himself in the big old manor house. Even though sometimes it was lonely and boring. Maybe it was time he tried his luck on the mainland scene again.

He decided to go to the mainland for dinner at one of the local bars and see if he could find someone who could erase the memory of Melissa from his mind. This would be a tall order to fill. However, he was on a mission.

Jimmy finished his preliminary plans to beef up security. He left the security shack late afternoon and headed to the Manor house. He gave Stella the night off from cooking dinner, then let her know he was going to the mainland to catch a bite to eat. She was happy her son was taking a much-needed break from the island.

When Jimmy got to the bar, facing indecision on whether he wanted to sit at the bar or at a table. Since his primary goal tonight was to erase the memory of Melissa from his mind, he decided on the table. It gave him a better vantage point to see the women in the bar.

There were plenty of attractive women. Most were in groups of 3 or more. There were also plenty of other men searching for their own match. This intimidated Jimmy. Being rejected by a woman in front of her friends terrified him. Vying for attention was not one of his strong suits. When the waitress came to his table, he ordered his dinner and a beer. He needed some liquid courage.

The beer came before his dinner, and he drank it rather quickly. By the time his dinner came, he was on his third beer, and he had the start of a good buzz. Then, having a clear view of the door, he noticed a couple more women walk in.

Shaking his head to get his vision clearer because he wasn't sure whether his eyes were playing tricks on him or he was experiencing a new type of beer goggles. There was no way beer goggles would make a woman look like Melissa, though. Could she really be here? He hadn't seen her in 7 years. Was his mind playing tricks on him?

The woman that looked like Melissa locked eyes with him. Those amber brown with flecks of golden eyes had a flicker of recognition in them towards him. Then there was the sheepish smile and a small wave. It was her. Now she was walking towards him. His heartbeat fast in his chest, and he hoped she couldn't tell.

"Hey, Jimmy, long time no see. How are you doing?"

Melissa leaned on his table with both arms.

He couldn't believe she was right here. His hands slipped onto his legs under the table, wiping the sweat off his palms and pinching himself. He realized he was not dreaming. Shockingly, the one person he was trying to forget was now facing him. But how could he ever forget her? Her flowing dirty blonde hair and her dimpled cheeks when she smiled.

Was it the alcohol, or was he still profoundly attracted to her? He honestly couldn't tell. All he knew was it was taking every ounce of restraint for him not to gather her up in his arms and kiss her. But, at least he had sense enough to know that would probably not turn out too well for him.

"*Oh, hey, Melissa. Yeah, really long time. I am doing well. How the heck are you doing?*"

Jimmy acted nonchalant.

"*I am doing really well. I am working on my doctorate in psychology now. Dad and Zach told me you are head of security on the island and living in the Manor house. That's quite an accomplishment.*"

"*Yeah, the new owners didn't want to live in the Manor house, and they didn't want it left empty, so they offered to let me live there. Kind of like extra compensation. Your father and brother didn't say you were coming for a visit.*"

"*They don't know I am here. Could you be a doll and not tell them you saw me, please?*"

"Sure, I guess. Why wouldn't you want to see your family, though?"

"I refuse to step foot on that cursed island! I don't understand why anyone would want to stay there. If I told them I was out here with friends, they would guilt me into going to see them. I have worked hard to distance myself from the shadows of that place. No way do I want to go back."

"That's too bad. There are many people who miss you and love you there."

"As much as I miss the people and love them too, I need to preserve my sanity and my life. It's been good catching up with you, Jimmy. I hope you continue to be well. I need to get back to my friends."

Melissa finished speaking and turned to walk away. Not knowing what came over him. Jimmy scrambled out of his chair and caught up to her, gently grabbing her arm and turning her to face him. It shocked her when he embraced her and passionately kissed her. Jimmy didn't want to let go, and he certainly didn't want to stop kissing her. The taste of her sweet lips again rekindled the smoldering fire within him that had been burning for so long. Melissa wasn't resisting and actually seemed to melt into his embrace.

He ended the kiss and looked her in the eyes.

"When you are ready to come back to the island and be my wife. I will be waiting."

Jimmy let go of Melissa, put a hundred-dollar bill on his table to cover his check, and walked straight out of the bar. He couldn't believe he had just done that. Boldness had never been part of his repertoire. *Did I just ask Melissa to marry me?* He thought to himself.

Melissa just stood there, mouth agape, watching Jimmy walk out the door. *Did he just ask me to marry him?* The kiss had stirred up old feelings she had fought for seven years to repress. Then, her friends came up to her, asking her many questions about Jimmy. She quickly told them he was an ex-boyfriend and then continued her evening out.

It wasn't until later she replayed the interaction with Jimmy in her head when she was lying in bed. *Damn it, Jimmy, why did you have to kiss me?* She remembered how he took charge and went after what he wanted at that moment. She just wished he would leave the island and go after what he wanted, clearly her.

She hadn't resisted his kiss. In that instant, she didn't want it to end. It had transported Melissa back in time in that brief minute. Earlier in their lives, all she wanted to do was be with Jimmy and love him.

Tonight taught her one thing. She still loved him, and she knew he still loved her from his actions. Now the only problem was figuring out what to do about it. She would not be returning to the island. That was a definite no for her. So, the only solution was convincing him to leave the island. That would be almost impossible. She fell asleep dreaming of being in Jimmy's arms once again.

Chapter 6: Sisters

With the obnoxious beeping of her alarm clock, Jessica rolled over and begrudgingly turned it off. She hadn't slept well after the nightmare. She rubbed her eyes to help wake herself up. Jessica realized how much she hated waking up without Timothy by her side. Her sister Samantha was stirring in the other twin bed in the room. Jessica could tell she wasn't a fan of alarm clocks, either. The pillow was being used to cover her head.

They both knew they needed to get up and get dressed. First order of business for the day, the girls had a breakfast date with their mother and grandmother. Then they were all going to head to the dress shop to pick out Jessica's wedding gown.

Jessica was not looking forward to shopping. She rolled over on her back and pulled the covers over her head. Procrastination was her superpower when she really didn't want to accomplish a task.

Samantha slowly got out of bed herself and got motivated. The more she moved around the room, her excitement built. She looked forward to helping her sister pick out her wedding dress. Something that Samantha had never thought would happen a few months ago. But, when she found out she had a big sister, the feeling of winning the lottery overcame her.

Samantha jumped on the twin-sized bed her sister was lying in with the covers over her head.

"Rise, and shine, sleepyhead! Today is the

day you say yes to the dress!"

Jessica just groaned, throwing the covers down off her head. Then she saw her younger sister with her hands and knees on the bed bouncing with child-like excitement. This made her smile and bust out laughing.

She had never had siblings before. This was all new, and she felt as though both were catching up on the things in childhood they never got to experience together. A light bulb went off in her mind, and in one swift movement, she sat up and grabbed her pillow. A little more vigorously than she expected, swinging and knocking Samantha off her bed with the first hit. Samantha grabbed her pillow and retaliated.

They both became breathless with laughter and the exertion of the pillow fight. Jessica felt less anxious and tense afterward. She could perceive the excitement of the day that had been radiating off her sister.

When they came bounding down the stairs together, they found their mother and grandmother waiting for them. Mira just smiled at them both as she could see that bond growing between her two daughters. She felt blessed that their family had finally become whole after not having Jessica with them for so many years. Their grandmother just looked at them scornfully.

"It's about time."

Jessica and Samantha brushed off her comment and didn't respond.

Mira looked at her mother.

"Mom, let the girls have their fun. We are not running late."

Kathleen Kennedy didn't appreciate frolicking or fun. She was a serious woman who only cared about status and prestige. In her eyes, her granddaughter's behavior was annoying. It seemed childish, and they weren't children. They weren't even teenagers. They were adult women. In her eyes, they should act decently.

When they got to the diner. Both Jessica and Samantha ordered a large stack of chocolate chip pancakes at breakfast. They smothered them with butter and maple syrup while their grandmother frowned in disgust. She had ordered scrambled eggs, toast, and two sausage links.

The girls giggled as they ate, daring each other to be the first to finish their plate. As they both struggled to eat all the pancakes, they joked that they would have difficulty trying on dresses with such full bellies. This did not amuse their grandmother at all, either.

Jessica finished all her pancakes, and Samantha ate about three-quarters. After using the ladies' room to wash up from the sticky syrup, they were on their way to the dress shop. The nervousness had returned to Jessica. She prayed everything would go smoothly.

The dress shop was a bridal boutique, one of those fancy shops with dresses and mannequins in the windows. They had an appointment, so they had the whole place to themselves. This was a saving grace for Jessica. She certainly didn't want anyone seeing her try on dozens of dresses.

Her mother and grandmother were already oohing and aahing over several big poofy princess-style dresses displayed on the racks. Finally, they both picked a dress for Jessica to try on. The boutique attendant was hyping up both dresses as beautiful choices. Jessica took the dresses into the dressing room. Samantha went inside with her to help her get into them.

As Jessica slipped into the first one and looked in the mirror at herself, she suppressed a laugh and pursed her lips. This was definitely not her style. The sleeves were long and puffed up over her shoulders, starting just above her elbows. The scalloped neckline was uncomfortable, and the train was eight feet long. Bustled up, the train made her butt look twenty times bigger. It was hot and bulky, which would never work for a July wedding. She indulged her mother and grandmother and showed them the dress.

They gushed over her and the dress and said she looked perfect. The attendant also agreed with them. Thankfully, Samantha reminded them all it would be a July wedding, and this dress was not a practical choice. Reluctantly, her mother, grandmother, and the attendant agreed.

Dress two was just as horrendous. It, too, had long sleeves, although no poofy shoulders. The neckline went straight across. It had lace that went up and encircled her neck. She felt as though she was being strangled by itchy hands. This dress also had a long train that bustled made her butt look awkward.

Again, when she stepped out of the dressing room, her mother and grandmother loved the dress. This time, the attendant stepped up and reminded them of the season the wedding would occur. Samantha and Jessica sighed with relief that they didn't have to bring it up this time.

Jessica's mother, grandmother, and the attendant scrambled, looking for other dresses. Samantha helped Jessica out of the second dress and then looked for the perfect dress for her big sister. Finally, she found one that she thought would look elegant but simple for her sister. She brought it to the dressing room.

Looking at the dress on the hanger, Jessica could not believe Samantha had found the perfect dress. Now she was just praying it looked just as beautiful on her as it did just hanging there.

Stepping out of the dressing room in the third dress, she felt as if she was the center of the universe. Usually, that would make her uncomfortable. Notwithstanding, in this dress, it felt magical. She could walk, twirl, sit and just move, which felt absolutely fantastic in a dress.

Eyes watering, Mira covered her mouth with both hands. Jessica was elegant in the simple dress. Samantha had found the perfect one for her sister. Still, the dress wasn't a distraction from Jessica's natural beauty one bit. On the contrary, it only enhanced it one hundred percent.

Kathleen scowled. She felt the dress was too simple and a bit more revealing than a bridal dress should be. The attendant rebutted her and said that for a summer wedding, less was more.

Samantha beamed with pride at her sister in the dress she chose for her. It was perfect! No fuss, no muss, but absolutely elegant on her.

The dress was simple on the top, with three-inch sleeves off the shoulder and two straps coming up and over the collarbones. Two sides came together above the breastbone along the neckline, with a small broach. The bottom of the dress came up a few inches under the knee caps in front and tapered down around the legs to the floor behind.

With Jessica's long, curly, red hair flowing down over the white dress, it was a picture of simplicity and breathtaking elegance. This was the dress. When Jessica told the attendant it was the one she wanted, Samantha squealed and hugged her. Then, hugging her sister back, they both got misty-eyed.

Now it was time to pick out Samantha's maid of honor dress. Samantha wanted something simple like her sister. She definitely wanted to show off her long legs also. Jessica found a chiffon A-line scoop neck knee length cocktail dress with cascading ruffles in a sea-foam green and brought it to Samantha to try on. When Samantha slipped the dress on, she knew it was the one. It offset her long flowing red hair and her green eyes.

"It's perfect!"

"You look stunning!"

Jessica beamed with pride. Next it was her mother's turn to try on a long floral lace gown in sea mist with a beaded bodice. Both Samantha and Jessica were in awe at how radiant their mother looked in the dress.

"Wow, mom, you could pass as our older sister!"

Samantha agreed with Jessica's assessment of their mother. While Kathleen continued to disapprove of every choice they all made.

Finally, it was her grandmother's turn. After what seemed like an eternity, Kathleen settled on a sheath/ column gown with lace and elegant jewels sewn in the neckline. While she loved the color of lime green, Jessica cringed. The color seemed to clash with her grandmother's red hair that had started to show grey streaks. However it was what her grandmother insisted on and she let it go, pretending she loved it.

"That is quite an elegant dress there, grandma."

It was lunchtime when they finished. The women went out for lunch before heading back home. Jessica and Samantha were chatting about the wedding and various ideas for centerpieces in the back of the car. Then Samantha's phone buzzed, startling her, notifying her of an incoming text message.

As she read the message, she smiled and replied. Noticing the difference in her little sister's demeanor, the way her smile was radiating, and the twinkle in her eye, she nudged her sister's elbow. She didn't say a word to her. Samantha looked up from her phone, and Jessica nodded at the phone, smiling. She shrugged, mouthed the words, *"New guy friend."*

Jessica left her sister texting for the remainder of the car ride. She thought about all the sweet moments they had had that day. Two sisters who a few months ago never knew each other existed. Now bonded for life. Jessica couldn't imagine her life without her little sister.

When they were alone later back at the house, Jessica pressed her sister for more information on her new guy friend.

"So, tell me more about this mysterious guy you were texting throughout lunch today?"

"Well, for starters, I have known him for a few weeks now. He is one of my Thursday night regulars. He has always been shy, but this week he actually asked me for my number."

"And you gave it to him? Do you usually give your number out to strange guys at work?"

"Yes, I gave it to him. And, no, I have never done it in the past. He gives off a trust me vibe. So I did. We have been texting on and off since."

"Okay, so what else do you know about this guy?"

"His name is Zach Zimmerman. Are you

ready for some irony? He works with Jimmy on the security team on the island."

"Wait, what?"

Jessica was getting a red flag warning.

"He saw me at Alexandria's and Mary's funerals. Then he found out where I worked and drove up here on his days off, just to see me."

"That's kind of creepy and sweet at the same time. What else do you know about Zach?"

"He grew up on the island. He has an older sister who coincidentally dated Jimmy throughout high school. Unfortunately, she broke his heart and went off to college. She hasn't been back on the island since."

"Wow. There is so much we do not know about our cousin. So what does he look like? Give me the scoop, little sis."

"He is cute. His hair is this brownish-gold.

It's not cut short, more than a little above shoulder length, straight-ish and falls just so when he runs his hand through it. It's more of a tousled look. But, ugh, his eyes are to die for. They are brown with these flecks of gold."

Jessica watched her sister as she described Zach. This guy had her sister smitten already. She would have to interrogate Jimmy on him and make sure his intentions were pure with her little sister.

So much she had to remember for this week's meeting already. Foremost, she needed to find out if Allison or her brothers had a child 25 years ago. Next, she needed to find out that connection for Timothy. Then the discussion of her brothers moving into the Manor house with Jimmy needed to be brought up. And last, she needed to pull Jimmy aside and get the inside scoop on Zach.

The biggest thing, though, was she couldn't wait to get home and hug Timothy. Her dream had really shaken her up. Just thinking about it brought fear into her heart. She couldn't lose him. Not now. Never. The meaning eluded her. Should they postpone the wedding? Did her subconscious have cold feet? Maybe. Maybe not.

Chapter 7: Connections

Timothy made it home before Jessica returned from her trip. He had bought a bouquet of wildflowers at a gift shop in the airport. In a vase, he arranged them, placing them in the center of their dining room table.

He could not wait to see his beautiful bride-to-be. It had been a long week without her. The photographer who worked on assignment with him this time had grated on his last nerve. Her incessant talking in her squeaky voice while he observed and took notes drove him insane.

To top it all off, she had been immensely flirtatious towards him the entire trip. He didn't even think there would have been an attraction to her if he was single and drunk. Not that she was physically unattractive. Her personality irritated him too much.

This experience was the icing on the cake for him. He insisted Jessica do photography for all his assignments in an email he composed to his editor. Not sure how receptive to his demand his editor would be. He was willing to risk losing his career to make sure he stayed sane. Time away from Jessica for work and paired with other annoying photographers, had him at his breaking point.

He emailed and hoped for the best. He had a twinge of anxiety about how his editor would react in his gut. If he got canned, he could always just be a freelance writer. There were options for him, and he shouldn't have to back down from his convictions.

Jessica was not due to arrive home until early afternoon, so he checked his genealogy account while he was on his computer. There was finally a message from the second cousin match.

Dear Timothy,

Thank you for reaching out to me about our match. I am sorry for the delay in response. I tried to do as much digging as possible into the probability of you being part of my mother's side of the family. Since I know little about my father. I also have tracked down little information on my grandfather's family side.

I asked my mom if she knew any of her cousins giving up any children for adoption. She had no definitive answers. The only story about any of her cousins she could remember being a big deal was when her cousin Allison spent over a year in a psychiatric facility.

She didn't know why her cousin was there. All she knew was ever since, she had not been distant towards the family in general. Her cousin never married and had no children.

I wish I could give you more information that was helpful.

In the meantime, I would like to get to know you better since we are cousins. So maybe we can meet up soon and talk.

Your cousin,

Jack Martin

Timothy digested the message and then checked the family tree of this cousin. There was one Allison. The name rang a bell, Allison Simmons. Then he realized Cromwell Real Estate's CEO was Allison Simmons. She worked for Jessica. Could this be the same Allison? He sent Jack a response. Hopefully, he could get an answer quicker this time.

Dear Jack,

No worries about the delay in response. Thank you for the information you could provide. Every bit helps. I would absolutely love to meet up with you. It is cool to finally find a biological family member.

I have one question, though, about your mom's cousin Allison. I noticed her name is Allison Simmons in your family tree. Do you know her occupation? Also, my fiancée has an employee by that name. I am curious to differentiate if it is the same person.

Looking forward to your reply.

Your cousin,

Timothy

Patience waiting for a reply was going to

be the hard part. It had taken months for Jack to respond the first time. Timothy did not know how long it would take this time. He was about to log out of the site when he received a message notification. It was a reply from Jack.

Hey man, I actually do know her occupation. She makes a big deal of it at every family function she does attend. She is the CEO of The Cromwell Real Estate Development Company in Manhattan. Let's figure out when we can meet up. I live in New York City. Where are you living?

Timothy's heart pounded in his chest as he read the response from Jack. Jack's mother's cousin was the same Allison working for Jessica! This was mind-blowing to him. He quickly typed another message to Jack.

Woah! Small world! That is the same Allison who works for my fiancée. My fiancée takes the train from New London into the city every week for a meeting. We live in Connecticut. I could go with her, and we could meet for coffee somewhere while she was at the conference. If that works for you?

He couldn't believe it, the information possibly related him to Allison. The only way to prove or disprove being related to her would be through a DNA test. Timothy knew for sure Jack was his second cousin. The question was whether he was kindred through Jack's father's side of the family or Jack's mother's side. They would have to use the power of elimination. He would have to ask Jack if his mother would do a DNA test to see if a connection with Timothy was there.

Dude! Your fiancée is a Gardiner? How lucky are you? I work nights waiting tables, so anytime you are in the city, I can pretty much meet up. When is the next meeting?

Timothy laughed to himself, reading Jack's response. I guess he never really looked at Jessica as a Gardiner. Maybe because they didn't even know she was one when they first met. Jack's response woke him up to the realization that others probably look at Jessica the same way Jack does. The thought was kind of sobering. He typed his response.

Yeah, she is. Although, when we first met, she was not aware of it, neither was I. So it's a kind of weird twisted story. I can tell you tomorrow if you would like. That is when the next meeting is.

Timothy and Jack exchanged a couple more messages to solidify their plans to get coffee and meet the following day while Jessica was at her meeting. He was excited about connecting with his cousin. Finally, a biological connection to another person, something he had longed for his entire life.

His adoptive parents had never kept it a secret about his adoption. On the contrary, they had reminded him relentlessly that he should be grateful they adopted him. They acted like they were his saviors, and he should be eternally grateful. He was appreciative. The life they gave him had been good. Despite his physical needs being met, there was always that lack of connection. Not necessarily a lack of love, but a lack of proper bonding.

There was always that notion that he owed them everything for adopting him. But, as he got older, he grew to resent it. That had been the driving factor in finding out who his biological parents were. He craved connection and the bond between a parent and child. That he had never felt with his adoptive parents.

Timothy and Jessica had discussed this subject on numerous occasions since their introduction. She always expressed how truly blessed she felt growing up with her adoptive parents, the Greenhalls. She was always empathetic to him, though, knowing he did not have the same experience.

Thoughts of Jessica made him look at the clock. Any time now, she should be home. He couldn't wait to see her. She was his best friend and confidant. With the purr of her car coming up the driveway, he went out to meet her on the front porch.

Jessica noticed Timothy leaning against the post leading down the steps on their front porch. Her heart skipped a beat. She had missed him so much. A glimpse of him waiting there for her made her realize just how lucky she was to have him.

Putting the car in park and shutting off the engine. It startled her at how quickly he made it to her car door. Opening it for her, he helped her out of the car and embraced her. The kiss he planted on her lips reminded her of just how intoxicating he could be.

She felt drunk with desire for him and let her mind shut the rest of the world out. She rested her head on his shoulder as he scooped her up and carried her into their house. Drinking up his musky scent, she softly planted kisses along his neck.

They made it as far as the living room floor before succumbing to both of their desires. When they finished fulfilling each other, they rested in each other's arms and filled each other in on the events of the day.

Jessica listened intently as Timothy explained the conversation with Jack. She told him she had confirmed that Allison was the same Allison in the tree. But, having said that, Jessica didn't want to get him too excited. She explained that was why she had said nothing yet.

They pondered together the plausibility of Allison being his mother. She was the right age to have had him as a teenager, which would make sense of why she gave him up for adoption. It was Jessica who mentioned the story of being in a psychiatric facility could have been a cover for the pregnancy.

They recalled her own mother's cover story of having Mono, which kept her out of school with a homebound tutor. Both agree Allison's story might have been a cover story.

Either way, Jessica was thankful she knew this information before talking to Allison about Timothy. With the knowledge, she had to tread lightly on the subject.

Jessica told Timothy about her visit home. They discussed again how her brothers wanted to move to the island to help Jimmy.

"*I am a tad bit concerned that having the boys living on the island could be more of a hinderance than a help to Jimmy.*"

"*I see your point. I am sure Jimmy is capable though. Your brothers are capable too. Don't sell them short.*"

"*I know, it's just that nagging feeling about Mary's confession. It still bugs me. I don't want my brothers in danger. I just found them, I don't want to lose them."*

Then switching gears, she talked about the dress shopping experience, leaving details about the dress she chose out of the conversation. Timothy loved hearing the stories of her bonding with her sister. He laughed at the fact they were annoying her grandmother.

Then she talked about the guy. The one Samantha had been texting and how he was from the island. Timothy expressed some concern about the stalking aspect of how they met. Jessica explained how she was already going to get Jimmy's take on the situation.

Their stomachs both growled. They laughed. Getting back into the clothes that they had shed. They got some pizza from Village Pizza. It was one of their regular go to dinner spots when neither felt like cooking.

Timothy went to pick it up while Jessica unpacked from her weekend trip. She noticed the new flowers in the vase on the dining room table, smiling she walked over and inhaled their fresh fragrance. He always brought her flowers when he came home from a trip. It was a subtle way of saying how much he missed being away from her. His sweetness was so appealing to her.

They knew they had an early morning the next day, so they retired to the bedroom after dinner. Jessica slept so much better when he was home. She hadn't told him of her nightmare. Snuggled up on his shoulder with his arm around her, she quickly dozed off to sleep. Timothy listened to the even breathing of Jessica as she slept. He kissed her forehead, and then he dozed off to sleep himself.

Chapter 8: Meetings

Jimmy stumbled out of bed early on Monday morning. The room spun as he was still hungover from the weekend. The sight of Melissa had sent him into a tailspin. Saturday night, he had come home and drank more beers until he passed out. When he awoke Sunday afternoon, realized what he had done, and said to Melissa, he drank again.

The pounding in his head was made worse by every movement he made. Nevertheless, he knew he needed to get motivated. They expected him at the weekly meeting this morning. The face in the mirror he hardly recognized.

The stubble on his chin and jawline was

visibly dark. One side of his black hair was matted, while on the other side, it stood up. He splashed some cold water on his face, waking himself up a bit more.

After shaving and showering, he was feeling better. The aspirin he took was helping take the headache away. Even so, his stomach was rumbling for some sustenance. Liquid meals were not very sustainable.

Walking into the kitchen, Stella handed him a cup of coffee and a plate of scrambled eggs. He devoured the food faster than he had expected.

"Son, you look a little rough around the edges this morning. Are you okay to go into the city?"

"Yeah, Ma, I just need to shake this hangover."

"You haven't binged like that in a while, since

Melissa."

Stella's words trailed off. She hated to remind her son of that painful time in his life. Worry, though, ran through her mind. Almost losing him during that time. She didn't want to journey down that path again. Reflection made her realize they had been very close to losing their only son. The drinking had led to him trying to numb the pain of his broken heart with more potent drugs. Thankfully, they were able to get him the help he needed. Ms. Mary had helped get him into a better rehab facility. Finally, he had been able to get clean of the drugs. He still occasionally drank. This time he had really fallen off the wagon hard. The first for him. Concern about what set him off floated through Stella's mind.

"I know, ma, don't worry. I am okay. Just saw

someone I had been trying to forget."

"You saw Melissa?"

"Yeah, but you can't tell her parents, I promised."

"I won't tell, son. You know your secrets are always safe with me."

Jimmy filled in his mom about the chance encounter with Melissa and their interactions. It embarrassed him about the kiss and marriage proposal. Stella listened intently to her son explain what had occurred. Her heart broke for him. She knew he would never fully get over Melissa.

That connection ran way too deep. Stella filled a thermos of coffee for him for his trip into the city. He kissed her forehead and headed out the door.

Jessica and Timothy woke up early,

gathered their things for the day, and headed to the train station in New London. This had become Jessica's weekly routine. However, Timothy had rarely joined her.

It was a pleasant change of pace, having him to talk to along the way. They both had fun people watching. Timothy had fun making up things about the people they were watching.

A woman possibly in her thirties or forties sat across from them talking loudly on her cell phone. Timothy speculated she was a spy using reverse psychology to bring attention to herself in order to blend in. Jessica joined, and it filled the entire morning with laughter and speculation between them.

When they made it to the office building, they kissed and parted ways. In the coffee break room, Jessica ran into Allison, preparing herself a cup of coffee. Jessica contemplated how to bring up Allison's potential relationship with Timothy. It was Allison, though, that struck up a conversation first.

"Was that your fiancée this morning?"

"Yes, that's Timothy. He also has a meeting."

"Very handsome. You are lucky. What does Timothy do for work?"

"Yes, and I feel blessed to have him in my life. He is my world. He is a writer for National Geographic. That's how we met. We worked together on the Gardiners Island story."

"Ah, sounds exciting. What type of meeting is he having here in the city?"

"Oh, it's not for work. It's actually a personal meeting. Ironically, being adopted, he just recently got in contact with a second cousin that he matched with on a genealogy website."

Jessica was observing Allison and her re-action.

"Wow, that's crazy that you are both adopted! I hope your fiancée has a good meeting with his newfound cousin."

"What is crazier is we both share the same birthday!"

"Really?? What day is that?"

"June 7th, 1992."

Allison had just taken a sip of her coffee. She seemed to choke on it and started cough-ing.

"Are you okay, Allison?"

"Yes, thank you. The coffee was just hotter than I expected."

She then promptly left the room.

Noticing that Allison had left her coffee cup on the counter in her hurry to leave, Jessica dipped her pinky into it. It was lukewarm. She thought this was interesting. That meant her reaction was to Timothy's birthdate and not to the coffee.

The board meeting discussed the preliminary cost analysis of the demolition and rebuilding or just remodeling of the existing building they had recently gained. It showed that the costs saved by repurposing far outweighed rebuilding costs. Jessica felt good about asking for the cost analysis. The findings were surprising to Allison.

"It may cost us less to remodel, but in the long run, new is going to give us a bigger resale value."

"Honestly, Allison, no one can predict the market and resale value. You may find a client that cherishes the older architecture. Someone like me. Given the chance and choice, I would re-

model all the old buildings to preserve the past."

The board decided to remodel the building to preserve the exterior architecture. Asbestos remediation comes first. After it was finished then discussion would continue. Not knowing if unknown costs will add to the project.

When the board meeting finished, Richard, Jessica, and Jimmy stayed in the conference room to have their private consultation. Richard brought up the question of Richard Jr. and David moving onto the island permanently to live in the Manor house along with Jimmy.

The hair on the back of Jimmy's neck bristled at the request. Not because he didn't want to share the island with his cousins, he was just concerned about their safety. He had kept his concerns about Mary's death a secret until this point. He had also thought it was prudent to keep the deer carcass incident a secret. *Should I tell them?* He thought to himself. Jimmy decided not to voice his concerns.

"I could definitely use the extra manpower on security. We always feel understaffed. If they will help, I gladly will welcome them into the ranks of the security team. I also wouldn't mind the company in the manor house. That big old place gets lonely."

He did need the extra help with the security. Having them help, whereas they were vested in the island, could be beneficial.

There wasn't much else to discuss with the island. Richard left to return to Boston. This left Jessica and Jimmy alone in the conference room. Out of respect for her sister's privacy, Jessica had not asked about Zach in front of her father.

"Hey Jimmy, what do you know about Zach on your security team?"

"He is a good guy. I have known him my whole life. I trust him. If this is about him talking to your sister, I already warned him."

"I hope you are right. Samantha is already head over heels for him. I don't want her heart getting broken."

"By the smile on his face when he was texting her Saturday, the feeling is mutual. I don't want Samantha to suffer the consequences of heartbreak, either. Personally, I know what that is like."

"Zach told Samantha about you and his sister. I am sorry she broke your heart."

"Yeah, me too. Me too."

Jimmy and Jessica finished their conversation and parted ways. Jessica was excited to find out how Timothy's meeting with Jack went. As she was leaving, she bumped into Allison again.

Allison seemed a bit distracted. Her standard self-control and composure were shaky, and Jessica wondered if the board siding with her and not Allison caused it.

"Hey Allison, I hope the outcome at the board meeting today didn't upset you. I know you are for new construction. I hope there are no hard feelings?"

"Not at all. After seeing the cost savings, it's the better business decision, short term. I am just not sure it's the wisest decision for long-term investment. Researching Dublin, I see what you mean about the artistic blend."

"Okay, I just didn't want to step on your toes

or upset you. I value you here. I don't want to do anything to lose you."

"I appreciate you saying that. My mind is elsewhere today. No worries though, I will get myself back on track."

"Actually, I noticed. That is why I am concerned. If you ever need to talk. About anything, I am here for you."

"Thank you. I will keep that in mind."

Jessica left the office building and went to meet up with Timothy. She hoped Jack was still with him. It was exciting to her to meet a biological relative of Timothy's. Then a terrible thought crossed her mind. *What if it didn't go well?* Anxiety built inside her.

Rounding the corner, she saw the coffee shop the meeting was taking place at. A little more reluctantly, she entered the shop and looked for Timothy. He was sitting, laughing, engrossed in friendly conversation with the man across from him. She really didn't want to interrupt.

Timothy looked her way. He stood up and motioned for her to join them.

"Jessica, this is my cousin, Jack."

"It is a pleasure to meet you, Jack. I am so excited for you both!"

Jack shook her hand when introduced.

"It is great to meet you too! Timothy has told me about you. I really can't believe how you too met."

"Yeah, definitely not your run-of-the-mill romance story. We didn't swipe left or right. Destiny, same place at the same time."

"Well, to be honest, it wasn't just destiny. I knew Arthur, and he knew I was a big fan of

your photography. With Alexandria's urging, he recommended you to me and my editor for the Gardiner Island story. I didn't know it was all part of Alexandria's plan, though."

"Wow, still amazing! I guess I can admit I am awestruck. I have never met a millionaire before."

"I don't look like one and I certainly do not act like one. Probably because I didn't grow up as one. Just treat me like you would any other human being, please. We are family now. Or at least when Timothy and I get married. You two look so much alike."

The resemblance was uncanny. Jessica commented they could pass as brothers. They laughed and agreed.

They talked about so many things that Jessica's head was spinning. Jack explained he had told Timothy that his mother had agreed to do a DNA test through the genealogy web-site. To help them narrow down which side of Jack's family Timothy was a part of. This news made Jessica so happy for Timothy.

Jessica filled them both in on the conversation with Allison and how she was acting differently afterward. They both agreed that it made things suspicious of her. They all held the same view. Since they didn't know the reason behind her psychiatric hospitalization, there could be a logical explanation.

It was getting late by the time they said their goodbyes. They made plans to meet up the following week. Timothy and Jessica headed to the train station to go home.

It had been a productive day. Jessica had swayed the board to vote along with her idea, which impressed Timothy. The discussion also included the decision to allow the boys to move in with Jimmy. Jessica also filled him in on her conversation with Jimmy about Zach and Samantha.

It was late by the time they got home. They wanted to climb into bed and get some sleep. As Jessica lay nestled against Timothy, she looked up into his eyes. It surprised her to see a tear welling up in the corner.

"What's wrong?"

"Honestly, not sure. I am feeling overwhelmed right now. I am feeling nervous about finding my biological family."

"Oh, honey, I get it. I am right here by your side."

"I know you do. That helps so much. My fear is they will want nothing to do with me, like my adoptive parents."

Timothy choked out the last sentence. Jessica crossed her arm over his body and pushed herself up to look him in the eyes. He looked so vulnerable at that moment, and her heart just melted. She leaned over him and gently kissed his forehead. He reached around her and pulled her to him. Settling his head against her shoulder, he slowly stopped crying and started softly kissing her neck. They nurtured one another until they fell asleep in one another's arms.

Chapter 9: Darkness

The listening devices they planted in the Manor house came in extremely handy. They relished in the fact that Jimmy had spilled his guts to his mom about Melissa. Oh, how that would be used to their advantage in the future. The knowledge that Jimmy had fallen off the wagon was another vital secret. How the Gardiner family always fell right into their best-laid plans amused them.

Then, hearing that the two Gardiner boys were moving to the island and into the Manor house, was the icing on the proverbial cake. The family was making things just way too easy for them.

The excitement of what was to come was

building inside them. All the ways in which they could tear the family apart were swirling in their brain. Who to target first was a big question. They still didn't know. They needed more information about the family. Their comings and goings.

With Richard Jr. and David coming to stay on the island permanently, that would be much easier. Maybe one of them would be the first to go. The girls, though, would be fun targets. Easy to terrorize. Maybe even torture. One thing they knew for sure was in their mind. Jessica would be the last to go.

The hatred for her seethed in their veins. From the moment Jessica had stepped foot on the island, there was something about her that just irritated them. Her beauty was mesmerizing. Albeit, that wasn't it.

Aware of who she was, and that she was the heiress to the Gardiner fortune. That is what angered them. They had known about her for years and had worked hard to make sure she was not made aware of her heritage. How she came to the island was a mystery to them. It had to be orchestrated somehow. Who set her to the island was a conundrum. They didn't believe in coincidences.

Of course, they thought there were only two other heirs, Jessica and Jimmy, back only a few months ago. They knew the family secrets that even those two hadn't known about themselves. They thought back then, getting rid of them would have proven to be more accessible.

They had almost succeeded that first night in getting rid of Jessica. Oh, how it angered them that Timothy had interrupted them. They had stolen a pair of night-vision goggles from the security team. They had snuck into the bathroom where Jessica was bathing. Turned off the lights, locked the door, and had pushed her under the water. They had barely escaped through the passageway when Timothy had busted through the door.

He would pay for taking that kill away from them. He would pay dearly. Perhaps he could watch Jessica die, or maybe he would be the one to kill her, or even better would be to have her kill him. They just couldn't decide yet. They had time to make those plans. Either way, he would suffer the consequences of his actions.

The plans for the family's Christmas visit were coming along nicely. They had gained the boxes needed for the families' Christmas gifts.

Their imagination ran wild thinking about them all opening their packages on Christmas morning. It gave them such a rush.

Terror was their purpose for the gifts. Jessica had not heeded their first warning. The letter sat in a box, along with other items that would serve an essential purpose in the coming months. All that happened now was her fault. She should never have come back to the island.

Every life lost on the island, whether animal or human, was now her fault. They would make her feel the guilt. The thought of the darkness of guilt and shame enveloping Jessica made them feel jubilant.

A rumor went through the inhabitants about a deer carcass being mutilated and left to rot. Security felt it was someone that had snuck onto the island. They chuckled at the thought they had gotten away with another big kill. Right under everyone's noses, it emboldened them to do it again. They were waiting for it to be found.

It upset many inhabitants about the deer carcass. For most, it was such a violation of their way of life. They all embraced the Native American roots of the island. Respecting the land and the animals that lived on it. The inhabitants felt it had been a desecration. Not them though, they embraced a different aspect of the island's past.

They embraced the darkness. Early in life, their mother told them about the stories of dark witches who lived and worked on the island. They had descended from those bloodlines. Though their mother had never learned the craft, they had studied it. They were learning to perfect it and harness it.

Disgust filled them at the thought of their mother. Had she learned the craft and harnessed it, their lives could have been so different. They could have lived a life of privilege instead of a life of existence and servitude.

How else could they explain their lot in life? Being born to the mistress of the Manor house. Everyone knew their mother was promiscuous. What they didn't know was about her mistress status, though. Their birth known, their birthrights hidden. Their fellow inhabitants pitying them instead of respecting them.

When their secret becomes known, they will gain respect. The inhabitants would all know who they were, eventually. When they took their rightful place on the island. Revenge would be pleasant.

Patience was not their virtue. Still, they knew they needed to time things right to get away with what they were planning. They needed to make sure it pointed no fingers at them. The planning would point to someone else.

Christmas would be here soon. The entire family would be here. They could easily take them all out at once. Start a fire in the house when they were all sleeping. A tragic ending. There were too many variables in that plan, though. It would also destroy the house they couldn't wait to live in.

Richard's survival of the boating accident taught them that. His survival had also taught them that plans needed to be kept secret. No accomplices. Richard survived because he had heard the plans to kill him. Then, knowing the goals, he hatched his own survival plan.

The family could escape a fire. Too much risk, not enough control in the outcome. Picking them off one by one would prove more complex. Notwithstanding, there was the assurance that the family would disappear for good.

Each individual kill would strengthen them. The power they would gain would be great. More significant than any they had ever felt. They could do anything they wanted to. They would have it all.

They would have the island, the respect, the wealth, and with all that, they could find someone to share it all with. Maybe even love. They were sure they could make someone fall in love with them with all the power they would possess.

Everyone loved power. They had seen it their entire life. Those that didn't live on the island coveted those that did. Because of the perceived strength, the Gardiner family held. Their wealth and prestige gave them that power.

Other people with prestige had flocked to the island events. This was where they had observed the attraction to power that led to love on so many occasions. Maybe it was the love that led to the control. This thought had crossed their minds on so many occasions. Although they knew little about love at all.

Love was an enigma to them. They hypothesized it led to greater personal power only by observation. It was an emotion that had been barren in their life.

Even though they had never really felt loved, it was the one thing they craved more than revenge. To be accepted for who they were unconditionally by someone. They had never felt that from anyone. Not even their own mother.

Their mother seemed to despise their existence in this world. She lived her existence properly, serving the family during the day and at night serving entirely differently. So she was too busy to be a proper mother.

She gave no nurturing moments growing up. No, I love you, no bedtime stories, and no tucking them in at night. Instead, they pretty much raised themselves. A wild child roaming the island. Just learning about those that lived there.

Their father had nothing to do with them. He knew. It was inconvenient and messy to acknowledge them, though. So there was no love there, no nurturing, no relationship.

They were always an outcast. Until they were of age to be of use to those who owned the island. Then they had a job, as all inhabitants on the island did.

Learning their job, they performed it well. Using it to their advantage of observing and gathering secrets of the family. It gave them a wage and housing. Modern-day slavery in their mind. They would break those chains in time.

The inhabitants were second-class citizens. Especially when they ventured to the mainland. Everyone knew who were members of the Gardiner family and who were not. If you were family, you were royalty. If you were not family, you were trash.

It was rare that an inhabitant would find themselves treated fairly by mainlanders. However, it happened occasionally, and that was how some mainlanders found their way onto the island. First, becoming an inhabitant through marriage. Then, quickly becoming indoctrinated into the culture of the island.

Their match had yet to be found. They didn't fit in with the inhabitants or the mainlanders. They were a lone wolf. Hunting through the darkness to feel loved and accepted. To feel loved would be the most significant power boost ever.

Chapter 10: The Move

The week before Christmas, Jimmy was busy preparing for Richard Jr. and David to move in. He had updated the security team that their safety was the number one priority. They were going to be joining the security team as well. The pairing of Richard Jr. with Matt and David with Zach seemed good.

He had let Betty know to make sure all the rooms were clean and ready. Not knowing which rooms his cousins would choose to make their own, he wanted them all prepared. All except Mary's. It was the one room he had kept precisely the way it was when he first moved in. Not being able to bear the thought of anyone else occupying it yet.

Martin, the butler, was looking forward to the two Gardiner boys moving in. It was boring with only one person living in the Manor house. The years of dealing with Mary and her mood swings were long gone in his mind. He had enjoyed the change of pace with Jimmy and felt the addition of the other two males would bring some life back to the place.

He had felt outnumbered working alongside Stella and Betty in the Manor house for years. Especially after Richard had supposedly died. The only male in the house for too many years, he had become somewhat reclusive.

Now, though, he enjoyed shooting pool with Jimmy in the parlor most nights after dinner. The rapport they had made it fun to work for him. Martin had never felt that with any of the previous Manor occupants. Maybe it was different because Jimmy was just like him, still an employee of the Gardiners.

Jimmy had been rewarded, though, and allowed to live in the Manor house. Would that feeling of comradery disappear when the Gardiner boys moved in, though? That was his only fear.

The buzz around the island was filled with excitement and some anxiety. No one really knew the two Gardiner boys. Some of the older generations knew their father and had always held him in high regard.

When the moving truck pulled off the rickety ferry and drove up to the Manor house, everyone stopped what they were doing to observe the new residents. Two workers hopped out of the truck, and everyone went back to work, realizing they were not the boys.

Jimmy rode his ATV up to the truck and introduced himself to the movers. They explained the boys were coming across Gardiners Bay behind them in their personal vehicles. Since all could not fit on the ferry simultaneously, the boys had decided to go across last.

When the boys pulled up, Jimmy excitedly welcomed them home. He exchanged hugs with them both and patted them on their backs. He really hoped his trepidation did not show. There were still many reasons for him to be uneasy about this move. Their safety was first and foremost in his mind.

"Betty will show you the rooms available for you to choose from for yourselves. So please make yourself at home! As always, Martin will help you with your things and help you get settled. And, of course, Stella will have dinner prepared by 5:30

pm."

"*Thanks, Jimmy. David and I are both look-ing forward to shooting some pool after dinner! I am sure we are going to need the fun and relax-ation after moving all our stuff in.*"

Jimmy hopped back on his ATV and re-sumed his rounds while the boys followed Betty into the house to choose their rooms.

As they walked past Mary's old room, Betty gave a warning to them both.

"*Yous all should be mineful to stay outa thar. Mr. Jimmy don't want anyone goin' in and destur-bin' that room.*"

Richard Jr. and David looked at each other and just shrugged. They figured their cousin would have reasons for not wanting Mary's room touched. They would not question it one bit. Neither of them had any desire to enter it, anyway.

They still etched the gruesome scene they had witnessed months prior in their minds. They both chose bedrooms as far away from hers as possible. The movers had to first remove the existing beds and bureaus. Since they both had furniture they had brought with them.

It was easier for the movers to put the unused furniture into the attic than in the basement. When all was said and done, it was early evening. When the movers finished and the boys were settled in. They were looking forward to the delicious home-cooked meal Stella had been preparing. The aroma had been wafting throughout the house, making their stomachs grumble.

As Jimmy was heading back to the Manor

house to call it a day, he got a call from Zach on the radio to meet him and Matt out by the south end of Great Pond on the southern tip of the island. The shakiness in Zach's voice concerned him. It was rare that anything got Zach shaken up. He stopped quickly to let Stella know he would be late for dinner, not to hold things up, and headed to meet Zach and Matt.

It was dark, and their ATV lights were shining on what they had found. When he pulled up to the scene, Jimmy got the feeling of Déjà vu. It was another deer carcass. This time a doe. Killed the same way and mutilated. He took pictures, and they worked together to dispose of the body.

They worked silently together. They tried not to let the stench and decomposing body make them sick. Jimmy had hoped the first carcass was a fluke. Stupid teenagers pulling a prank or something. The discovery of this one made that scenario less likely. The timing couldn't have been less ideal.

The Gardiner boys had just moved in today. How was he going to keep this under wraps? He didn't want them to freak out. But, on the other hand, he certainly didn't need the family to back out of coming for Christmas, either.

"We have to keep this under wraps for a few weeks. You both understand, right? We can't have the family scared to come for Christmas. We may have to pull some double shifts, though, and increase patrols even more."

As Jimmy finished, he ran his hands over his face in frustration. He was mentally tired. His men were exhausted. They had beefed up patrols already after they found the first carcass.

"It's okay, boss. We will keep it under wraps, and we will do what needs to be done to keep everybody safe. Can I at least run some questions by Melissa about the type of person who might do this? She might be able to give us some insight. "

Zach looked at his boss sympathetically.

"That's a good idea, Zach. Your sister is a smart cookie. She might be able to give us a clue, Jimmy."

The mention of Melissa's name made Jimmy wince, but he knew Zach and Matt were right. She was smart. Psychology was the primary subject she was studying, and they needed some insight into the psyche of whoever was doing this.

"Mention the first carcass to her, not this one.

Everyone on the island knows about that one. Ask her hypothetically what it would mean if someone were to do it again. And tell her I said hi."

Zach said he would call her later that night. Concern was all over his face. He was just as determined as Jimmy to sort this out. They didn't know if this person posed a threat to any human on the island. Yet, they were taking it as a threat and would do everything in their power to make sure everyone was safe.

By the time Jimmy got back to the Manor house, dinner was over. Stella had made him a plate of leftovers, although he wasn't hungry at the moment. She could tell something was bothering him. Still, she didn't ask. His body language told her he was in no mood to discuss anything.

Joining the boys and Martin in the parlor,

Jimmy sat down to relax. They were already shooting pool and having a couple of beers.

"Hey David, aren't you a bit young for that?"

"If I was away at college enjoying the frat life, this is exactly what I would be doing."

David chugged the rest of his beer.

"Come on, Jimmy, have one with us! Let's celebrate our new brotherhood."

Richard Jr. threw another beer at David and one at Jimmy.

He caught the beer thrown at him. Jimmy knew he shouldn't drink it. He was not in the right frame of mind. His cousins didn't know about his past, so forgiveness could be given to them for their pressure. Not wanting to disappoint his cousins, he decided he could handle one.

They all enjoyed playing pool and hanging

out until late in the evening. Martin was the first to turn in. Jimmy followed suit shortly after. He knew the next day would bring a deluge of problems to solve because that was just how things were rolling lately. The boys would be introduced to the security team and start their training in the afternoon. The boys stumbled to bed as well.

All was quiet that first night in the Manor house. Then, in the morning, Jimmy's alarm jolted him awake. As he slipped out of bed, he kicked a couple of empty beer cans on the floor. He stopped in his tracks. One, that's all he remembered having. Cleaning up the cans, he assessed himself. No hangover, no headache, no feeling queasy, and no spinning of the room.

He shook his head. He shrugged it off as a joke by his cousins. Proceeding to shower and get dressed, then head down for breakfast, he would ask them about it later.

Jimmy had just finished his eggs, bacon, and coffee when he heard a bunch of yelling coming from upstairs. He went to investigate. Jimmy found both of his cousins in towels. As if they had both just gotten out of the shower standing in the hallway. Both were pointing to their bedrooms, visibly freaked out.

"What's the problem?"

"Dude, what the hell is that on my pillow? It wasn't there when I got up. It was there when I got out of the shower."

David was the first to say something.

"Same in my room! What the hell is going on? Is this some sort of sick initiation thing?"

Jimmy peered into David's room first. As he got closer, he knew what it was, and his heart sank. His stomach wanted to heave. The smell of formaldehyde was strong. There on the pillow was a heart. If Jimmy was a gambling man, he would bet that it came from a deer. As he went across the hall to Richard Jr.'s room and saw the same thing, he knew he was right.

He took pictures. He told his cousins he was sorry and would get to the bottom of this, then called Zach and Matt to the house. While his cousins went down for breakfast, they dusted for prints, took more pictures, and investigated as much as they could. Then they cleaned up the sheets. When they finished, Jimmy let Betty know both rooms needed new linens.

Before leaving for the security shack, he checked in on Richard Jr. and David to ensure they were okay. They both seemed less rattled than earlier, which eased Jimmy's mind a bit. As he left, he stopped in the kitchen to ask Stella if she had seen anyone in the Manor house that morning. The only person who generally wasn't in the place daily had been Samuel.

Samuel had fixed the dishwasher for her that morning. Then she remembered Betty had asked him to check out the washer and dryer while he was there, too. He had been in and out with tools and parts. Stella had been busy preparing breakfast, so she had paid little attention to his comings and goings. Nothing seemed out of the ordinary with him, though, she had added.

Leaving the Manor house, Jimmy paid Samuel a visit in his shop.

"Good morning, Samuel. What are you up to today?"

"Jimmy boy, I am working on this darned tractor again. It might be time to replace the old thing. Getting parts is harder and harder to come by."

"I heard you were up early fixing stuff at the Manor house this morning."

"Yeah, them women had me chasing issues they cause themselves. I know Stella is your Mom and all, but I have told her a million times she needs to rinse the dishes before putting them in the dang dishwasher. She is constantly clogging the thing up. Then that Betty. Geez, overloading the washing machine and not checking the lint trap on the dryer. You're gonna have a fire if you're not too careful."

Jimmy chuckled at Samuel's response. He

was never too fond of the womenfolk. They all seemed to annoy him regularly. His presence in the house that morning seemed on the up and up.

"You didn't happen to see anyone else in the house that normally isn't there, did you?"

"Nah, just the usual. Stella, Betty, and Martin. What's with the 3rd-degree boss?"

"Ah, nothing, just someone pulling some pranks on the Gardiner boys this morning. I am trying to figure out who is doing the hazing, so I can get them to knock it off."

"Not me, boss. I got too much to do around here than mess with those two. If I see anything out of the normal, I will let you know."

"Thank you, Samuel. I appreciate that."

Jimmy was perplexed. For the life of him, he could not think of anyone that would have done that to the boys. Then Jimmy got to thinking about the beer cans in his room. He had forgotten about them. *Did he drink more than one beer? Could he have blacked out?* It scared part of him to think he was heading down that dark road again. He needed to be more diligent and resist the temptation.

Chapter 11: Home Creepy Home

Timothy's phone rang. It was his editor. Timothy took a deep breath and steadied his resolve and thoughts before answering the phone.

"*Good morning Larry. What do I have the pleasure of your call today?*"

"*Timothy, my reasons for calling are twofold. First, I understand your frustrations with being away from your lovely bride-to-be for lengths of time. Second, I also understand she is the best at photography. I have no problem pairing you up with her for all of your future jobs. As long as she is not working on another project.*"

"*I appreciate your understanding, Larry. However, I also realize she is a freelance photog-*

rapher, and she may get work that conflicts with our deadlines."

"I am glad we could reach a mutual understanding, Timothy. I would hate to lose a talented writer. With that being settled, I have work for you and Jessica to do. Sorry, it is so close to the holidays and all."

After their conversation, he sent them both to Antarctica to do a piece on the hatching of Penguin chicks.

The assignment being so close to Christmas was annoying to Jessica and Timothy. However, they figured they could get the work done and be home just in time. It just meant that their investigation into Timothy's biological family would have to wait.

A consolation for them both was, they invited Jack to the family Christmas Eve gathering on Gardiners Island. Jack was excited to attend. Jessica had also asked Allison to attend the party under the pretense of working with Jimmy, Richard, and herself. Mentioning Arthur's invitation, hoping it would entice Allison to attend.

Before heading on their trip, Timothy researched the weather in Antarctica. Antarctica in December was bearable for Jessica and Timothy, who lived in New England. Average daily temperatures in the low 30s were not unheard of in New England, which was the norm this time of year in Antarctica. So they packed their winter gear along with their equipment and were on their way for an adventure.

The helicopter blades whirred above their heads as they hovered above the Scientific observatory camp they would call home for a few days. The brown tents and heavy machinery scattered around made the base look like a small military installment. They were showed both a cot and a footlocker to store their gear in the barracks. The mess hall was a small tent about 20 feet from the barracks. The latrines were situated around the back of the sleeping quarters.

Their accommodations took the wind out of their sails a bit. First, realizing they would not be bunking together. They bunked females on one side of the barracks and males on the other, with a fabric partition between them.

Then, the cuisine introduced some issues. The first night was less than ideal. The food presented was meatloaf, mashed potatoes, and green beans. It looked like canned dog food, something with the consistency of oatmeal instead of mashed potatoes and some green smoothie puree. The texture and taste were less than desirable. They knew they needed to eat, so they struggled to get some of it down.

Their first-morning meal was not much better, and they ate as much as they could stomach. Then, the two bundled up for the first expedition out to the penguin nests. They were ready in no time. Jessica and Timothy wanted to get this assignment over with as soon as possible. It was the harshest in terms of environmental conditions either of them had been on in a while.

The guide showed them the best vantage spots to observe the penguins hatching. He was doing his own scientific observations, so he stayed with them the entire day. All day, not a single egg hatched. This was the money shot Jessica was trying to get. She knew they couldn't leave until she got it.

It took three days of observing the penguins to catch the chicks' hatching. The shots Jessica captured of the chick's beaks emerging from the shells showed the miracle of their birth. She couldn't help but think it was ironic that these baby penguins were hatching for Christmas. The miracle of births always had a soft spot in her heart.

She looked over at Timothy and watched him write. Her mind wandered to the thought of them having their own children together. Soon, but not too soon. They would make great parents. At least, that was how she felt. She envisioned Timothy holding their baby for the first time and smiled. Timothy looked her way and caught her staring at him with love in her eyes.

"What is that grin across your face for?"

"I am just thinking of you holding our own baby one day."

"Are you trying to tell me something?"

"Oh, no, not yet anyway! You will be the first to know, though. After me, of course!"

They finished up their work for the day, laughing. It felt good getting what they needed for the assignment done. They were thankful they could leave the following day. This would give them a couple of days to develop the pictures and for Timothy to write the accompanying article. Then they would be off to meet the rest of the family on the island for the Christmas holiday.

Their first Christmas together. Jessica's first Christmas with her biological family. Timothy's first Christmas with his genetic cousin. There was so much to be excited about and thankful for. They kept talking about the gifts they had bought for family members the entire trip home. They couldn't wait for them to open them up Christmas morning.

Both of them felt the childlike excitement of the holiday again, which added to their over-all joyfulness. With the added motivation of the holiday approaching, Jessica and Timothy could get their assignment done in a day. The editor delighted in their work and how they had gotten it done in such a timely fashion.

Jessica got in touch with Jimmy.

"Hey, Jimmy. Timothy and I were hoping to come to the island a few days earlier than previously planned. Is that going to be okay?"

Jimmy briefly froze on the other end of the

phone.

"Sure. Why not? Your brother's are doing well and I am sure they will want to visit with you two for a couple extra days."

Jessica thought there was a slight hesitation in his voice. She shrugged it off as he was busy at work and getting everything ready for the rest of the family to arrive.

Delighted to hear that Arthur would join them for Christmas Eve, Jessica finished packing for their holiday getaway. Timothy packed his clothes and all the presents in the car, and then they were off to catch the ferry to Long Island.

The roads were snow-covered still from the minor storm that had pushed through the night before. Yet, sunshine glistened and sparkled off the snow-covered fields as they drove past. The untouched beauty was breathtaking.

The ferry service was running, despite being rougher than regular seas from the storm. They made it across the sound and headed towards the island ferry to cross Gardiners Bay. Jessica always dreaded that leg of the trip. The ferry was old and rickety. Jimmy was getting a replacement. Albeit, that would take time. Captain Bill always assured Jessica the vessel was seaworthy, rapping his knuckles on the bow.

Captain Bill was a little rough around the edges, with his long grey hair and beard, his weathered skin, and gruff voice. He wore a white captain's hat. A cigar was hanging out of his mouth. Not lit, he tended to just roll it back and forth in his mouth and chew on its end.

Growing up on the Island, his father had

been a captain as well. When he was sixteen, they had hired Captain Bill as a deckhand. Working under his father had toughened him up a bit. There was no favoritism on board his father's vessel, and he ran a tight ship. Captain Bill did the same.

As they pulled off the boat, they saw David on one of the ATVs alongside another security member. They waved as they passed him. His smile showed how happy he was. This delighted Jessica. David was the one she worried about the most. He was young and had no compass where he wanted his life to go.

When they reached the Manor house, it only took minutes for Martin to welcome them and start helping them unload their car. Jessica noticed the difference in his relaxed demeanor now compared to the first time she had been on the island. Although she also welcomed them, Betty was inside the house and was still stand-offish. Before unpacking, Jessica detoured into the kitchen to say hello to Stella.

As always, the kitchen smelled of delicious aromas. Stella gave Jessica a big welcoming hug and snuck her a few of the freshly baked Christmas cookies she had made. This transported Jessica back to her childhood as she bit into the cinnamon-covered morsel.

She remembered, closing her eyes, how her Mom made it an annual tradition for them to bake cookies before Christmas. They would start the day after Thanksgiving and bake daily until Christmas Eve. They boxed up many cookies and gave them as gifts to friends and neighbors. A tiny teardrop escaped from the corner of her eye. Quickly opening her eyes and wiping the tear away, she thanked Stella for the cookies and headed to her room to unpack. Stella gave her a nod and squeezed her hand.

Martin and Timothy were just finishing bringing the bags to the room. They were talking about playing pool later after dinner. The atmosphere in the Manor house had gone through a significant overhaul since the last time she was here. The air of gloom and doom was gone. Hope and happiness replaced it.

The two places in the house that still gave her the creeps were the room she had stayed in the first time. The one someone almost killed her in. Also, Mary's room. Just walking past it gave her the chills and brought her memory back to that fateful morning.

Her thoughts went to Betty. It must be difficult for her to work day in and day out and walk past that room. She was the one who found Mary. Jessica was kicking herself for not realizing this earlier. She made a mental note to discuss it with her father and Jimmy when she got a chance. That could explain Betty's demeanor.

After unpacking, Timothy and Jessica had some time to explore the Island. Something they had yet to do. They got a couple of ATVs to do some riding. They met Samuel in the garage.

"Hi, Samuel. We are going to do some exploring with two of the ATVs. Which two should we take?"

"Those two over there are ready to go. Be sure to make sure everything works before you head out, though. We don't want any accidents occurring."

Samuel pointed his thumb over to two of the ATVs.

"Thank you. We will make sure the machines are working," Timothy said, a little more annoyed than he should have shown. *"Even though that's your job."*

Neither of them had an affinity towards Samuel. They got the impression the feeling was mutual. He hadn't been friendly towards them the first time they met, and his attitude hadn't seemed to change.

Jessica felt it was best to follow the trails already blazed through the snow by the security team. She didn't want to get stuck somewhere on the island, not knowing how to get back to the Manor house.

Heading east from the Manor house, they followed a path that took them southeast and

over Willow Brook pond. They found themselves at Two Lookout Tower. Jimmy was there
and welcomed them. Showing them the view
from the lookout tower, it amazed Jessica
as the beautiful waves of the Atlantic ocean
crashed along the coast of the eastern beaches.
The power that the waves displayed was spec-
tacular.

Jimmy's radio crackled, making them all
jump out of the quiet watchfulness they had
been in. The voice on the other end was informing him he needed to meet them at Captain Kid Hollow. Jessica thought she recognized the voice as her brother Richard Jr., as
Jimmy hopped on his ATV to meet up with the
person on the other end of the radio. Jessica
and Timothy got on their ATVs and followed
suit.

When he pulled up to Richard Jr. and Matt at Captain Kid Hollow, Jimmy could tell by the look on their faces it wasn't good news he was being called out there for. He got off the ATV and walked up to them to another deer carcass. It was another doe mutilated, just like the others.

Jimmy rubbed his face with both his hands. He had already told David and Richard Jr. about the other carcasses after they found the hearts on their pillows that first morning. With Timothy and Jessica right behind him, he knew he would have to inform them of everything that had occurred.

Timothy hopped off his ATV, followed by Jessica. When they saw what the commotion was all about, they both stood with their mouths open. They were both accustomed to the views of nature. They had never been exposed to such grotesque disregard for life. Jessica was the first to lose her stomach contents, with Timothy following suit.

Jimmy coaxed them both to head back to the Manor house as it would get dark soon. He promised he would fill them in when he got back. But first, the security team would have to do a thorough investigation.

When Jessica and Timothy returned to the Manor house, they went straight to their room. Disconcerted by what they witnessed, Jessica paced.

"What the hell was that? Who the hell would do such a thing?"

"I don't know, hun. Jimmy will have some answers when he gets back."

"I sure do hope so! Did you notice how none

of them seemed phased by it? Like it was an every-day occurrence or something?"

"Yeah, I did. The entire security team was all eerie calm. Even your brother."

"I have seen dead deer before. Hell, I have killed plenty, but that. That was a blatant disregard for that animal's life."

"Let's try to forget it for now till Jimmy comes back."

Timothy trailed off his sentence as he wrapped his arms around Jessica and just hugged her tight. She relaxed a bit and leaned her head on his shoulder.

"I will try, but just when I thought the creepiness of this place was gone, it goes and rears its ugly head again."

Chapter 12: Good morning, surprise!

Jimmy and the boys got to the house for dinner. They looked ragged and drained. Jessica let them eat dinner in peace without asking the nagging questions in her mind. It wasn't until later in the evening, when they were all relaxing in the parlor, Jimmy started the conversation.

"Hey Jessica, I need to say I am sorry first. I have been keeping some stuff from you and your father that has been occurring on the island. At first, I thought it was just some punks pulling sick pranks, in my defense. Until your brothers got here, and the targeting occurred."

"Wait, what? My brothers were targeted? How? By who? When you say targeted, do you

mean like I was targeted?"

Jessica's mind was racing. She had known in her gut Mary wasn't the one that had targeted her before. Despite her confession in her suicide note. Was Jimmy confirming that suspicion?

"Look, I don't know who. That is the most frustrating aspect of this whole thing. I have interviewed everyone on this island half a dozen times casually to not raise suspicion with any of them. No one gives me clues as to be able to do this. None give any inclination of dislike to the Gardiner family. On the contrary, they are all grateful for their livelihoods here. With no motive why someone would do these things, and no evidence leading to a suspect, my hands are tied."

"I got one question, Jimmy. And I want a straight-up honest answer. Do you think this is the same person who was targeting me before?"

"Yes. Forgive me for keeping that from you, too. I investigated the theory of Mary using the passageway to get away after almost drowning you. There was no way she could do it and re-appear in time. None. Things had been quiet, though, so I figured things were good. I am sorry."

"Hey, it's okay. But, yeah, am I a little freaked out. Absolutely. No one in their right mind wouldn't be. I trust you, and I know you are doing everything in your power to keep everyone safe and understand all this."

Jimmy took a deep breath in and released it, relaxing his shoulders a bit. They all agreed to keep all the incidents from Jessica's parents and Samantha. At least until they knew more. They were soon forgetting all about the latest find and playing pool.

Martin joined them, and they all had a few beers. Being cautious about drinking still, Jimmy set his mind on only having one. He held onto the one can all evening. Only putting it down when it was his turn to shoot pool.

When it was time to turn in for the evening, Jimmy marked his can before putting it in the recycling bin. Then, up in his room, he made sure there was no single can of beer empty or full anywhere. He even opened the little parsonage cabinet on the wall. There was not a drop of alcohol in his room.

This had become his nightly routine, and every morning he awoke to the same thing. Empty beer cans strewn over his floor, and no memory of him drinking them. He checked them for fingerprints every time, using the primary dusting and lifting with tape method.

The ones he found always seemed to be his.

Of course, he kept all of this secret and didn't ask anyone else to analyze the prints. He didn't want anyone to know that he was afraid he was relapsing somehow and not remembering anything. He had heard of psychosis causing memory loss. Using alcohol and drugs could induce psychosis.

He had a few episodes of psychosis after drug and alcohol use in the past. It was what led him to get treatment. He had been suitable for so many years. The thought of him relapsing without knowing scared him. However, he didn't know who he could reach out to for help. He fell asleep after tossing and turning for what seemed like hours.

Morning came, and Jessica was the first to rise. She left Timothy sleeping and padded down to the kitchen. Stella was already making breakfast, stopping to make Jessica a cup of tea. Jessica loved Stella. She was always so cheerful and seemed to love cooking for everyone.

Betty came into the kitchen and seemed to be less than amicable.

"Stella, ya know if Samuel is out in thar shop yet? That danged washer's acting up again."

"I saw the light on when I walked past this morning, Betty. Get your coat and boots on and go see if he will come and fix it for you again."

Grumbling something about the cold, Betty followed Stella's instructions and headed towards the shop to get Samuel. Stella looked at Jessica.

"That girl is always breaking that machine. Samuel is going to throw a fit again. He is never happy when he has to tinker with stuff in the

house. At least since Ms. Mary's passed. I think he had a soft spot for her. He never minded fixing things when she was here."

"Is that so?"

Betty was back in the kitchen, with Samuel following right behind within twenty minutes. Stella was right about one thing. Samuel did not seem amused at having to fix the washing machine again. As he walked through the kitchen and into the utility room, he grumbled under his breath.

Jessica couldn't hear what was being said between Betty and Samuel. She could tell that it wasn't a friendly conversation. Betty emerged from the utility room and stormed off to do her housekeeping duties.

Timothy was just entering the kitchen and was almost knocked over by Betty's departure.

"Wow, someone seems to have woken up on the wrong side of the bed this morning!"

"Ah, the washing machine is broke, again. Samuel is trying to fix it. But, despite that, he isn't too pleased to be tasked with the job."

Jessica shrugged.

Laughing, Timothy leaned over and kissed Jessica on the forehead.

"Sounds like an old married couple."

Samuel emerged from the utility room as they both laughed at Timothy's comment. Grumbling again, something about needing to go find Betty and apologize. This time, it seemed like something was wrong with the blasted machine and not operator error.

Stella pointed him in the direction Betty had gone. While Jessica and Timothy sat at the island in the kitchen eating their breakfast, Jimmy was upstairs staring at the empty beer cans on his floor.

He had woken up hours ago, or at least that is what he thought. The appearance of the cans again was making him seriously question his sanity. His focus was trying to figure out how this kept happening. There were no physical signs he had drank more than the one beer. No hangover and no after-effects. Could he be sleepwalking and drinking?

So entrenched in his own thoughts, he hadn't heard Jessica leave her room across the hall. He also didn't hear Timothy go a while later. Not even hearing Betty stomping through the hallway while doing her morning housekeeping duties. Or Samuel tracking down Betty and apologizing. Instead, Jimmy was lost in his own mind, trying to figure out if he was going crazy or not.

When Jessica and Timothy returned to their room, they had been surprised to see the bed already made. They figured Betty must be in a frenzy this morning to get her work done. So Jessica got ready to take a nice relaxing bath and get dressed.

As she pulled back the shower curtain that surrounded the claw-footed tub, she jumped backward, finding what appeared to be a heart in the bathtub.

"WHAT THE HELL IS THIS?"

Her yelling snapped Jimmy out of his fog. He rushed across the hall to see what his cousin was hollering about. As soon as he looked in the tub, his stomach dropped. They called security to investigate, and Jessica and

Timothy moved to an unfamiliar room so they could get showered and dressed in privacy.

The thoughts running through Jimmy's head were getting darker and more suspicious. He was questioning whether he was the one doing all these strange things. Could he be experiencing blackouts? Both his biological parents had been capable of murder. Could he have inherited those psychotic traits?

Another thought came rushing to his mind. Could he have been the one to almost drown Jessica? He felt like he was indeed going crazy. Fear gripped him. Was he a danger to those around him? Should he try to get some professional help? He didn't know what to do.

So he did the only thing he knew how to. He investigated the scene as thoroughly as possible. He interviewed everyone who had been in the house at the time of the discovery. But nothing was revealed to point him in any specific direction.

The lack of clues and evidence just added to his dread. Rousing from his thoughts when Zach started asking questions.

"Hey boss, you know, Melissa said that whoever is doing these things is a psychopath. Do you think they are going to hurt the family? Are the hearts some type of warning? The hearts were only presented to members of the Gardiner family. Wouldn't that point to them being targets?"

Jimmy hadn't heard Zach talk so much in his life. He rubbed his hands over his face and tried to answer his questions as best he could.

"Yeah, I know that's what you mentioned she had said. But, honestly, I don't know the answer to any of those questions. I am just as confused

as you are. You bring up a point I hadn't thought about, though. There might be some sort of symbolism in the heart. We should look into that."

Was the family in danger? That was the big question. Jimmy could not ascertain the answer at the moment. There had been no direct threats. Did it appear the family was being targeted? Absolutely. By who, though, was the big question he could not answer.

There was no motive for anyone to target the family. He was the only member of the family not known about. Was that why he had not been targeted? He was contemplating calling off Christmas. He needed to talk to Jessica, Richard Jr., and David to get their thoughts.

"Samantha is coming today, boss. Is she going to be targeted next?"

"I don't know. There have only been three

deer carcasses found, so only three hearts. Unless this sick bastard has another one stashed somewhere, she may be in the clear. Let's make sure we triple-check the island today, all remote areas. If we find a carcass, we know that the heart will be used to torment Samantha. We need to prevent that from happening."

"I will volunteer for 24-hour bodyguard duty."

"I am sure you would."

Jimmy laughed at Zach's suggestion, but he thought it might wind up being the best possible answer at the moment. They discussed the possibility of twenty-four-hour bodyguard protection for the entire family as well. This was something they had never had to do on the island.

However, they realized they needed to sit

down with the others before implementing this. So they headed downstairs to round up the Gardiner siblings to have a frank discussion about the security threat they were facing.

Jessica and Timothy were still edgy about the heart in the bathtub sitting in the parlor. Part of Jessica just wanted to pack her things and leave the island for good. The creepiness had returned, and she no longer felt safe. Deep in her gut, she knew they were all sitting ducks.

Jimmy and Zach came into the parlor and sat down. Richard Jr. and David, who had been getting ready for work, joined them. Jimmy took a deep breath and then addressed them all.

"I think by now we all realize this is not a prank. I think we all know we are dealing with

some sick psychopath. What we don't know is what their end game is? We don't know why they are doing these things? And we certainly don't know who is doing it. Zach and I discussed the possibility of round-the-clock bodyguard protection as an added security measure for all family members. The only problem is we are already short-staffed. It would leave aspects of the island vulnerable. Patrols in the remote areas would stop. Today, though, we are going to step those up. If we find another carcass, we know the next step would be to target a family member. Most likely, that would be Samantha since she was coming today. Thankfully, your parents aren't arriving until tomorrow evening. Hopefully, we can piece together what is going on here and keep everyone safe."

David was the first to respond. He seemed eager and excited to express his opinions.

"I know it isn't a short-term solution, but I think we need to install cameras. Using a drone to search the island could also be beneficial. In the meantime, I agree with the suggestion of bodyguards. I could order the cameras today. No idea when they will get here, but I could install them when they do. I already have a drone. It's upstairs in my bedroom. I could use it today to search the island."

"Wow, great ideas, kid! Get that drone and get searching! Order those cameras, get as many as you think we need. Also, I need someone to research what those hearts may mean. Could there be symbolism somewhere?"

"Timothy and I can do some research on symbolism. I agree the bodyguard system might be needed. Let us see what the rest of today brings. Maybe we can figure it out together. In the meantime, we should not tell Samantha or Mom and Dad about any of this."

"I am going to head out on the ATV and do a more thorough search of remote areas. Then I will start up north and go back and forth. I will see if I find anything. David, radio me if you see anything suspicious with the drone," said Richard Jr.

"I will start at the southern end of the island and do the same thing," said Zach.

"Sounds like we have a plan. Keep in radio contact at all times. I will search the middle of the island. Let's make sure this son of a bitch can't mess with us anymore," Jimmy ended the conversation.

Chapter 13: The Date

In researching the symbolism of the animal hearts, Jessica and Timothy found out that some forms of black magic or voodoo used them in rituals of revenge or vengeance. So they deemed it a threat.

David flew the drone over the entire island, going low in specific places to ensure he saw nothing. No dead deer carcasses anywhere to be found. He felt a little more at ease. Through the drone, he saw a herd of deer in a field. He flew it down to see how close he could get. It amazed him at how trusting the deer were. The drone got within inches of them before they got scared off by the noise it made.

Richard Jr. made a pattern of back-and-forth paths on the northern part of the island and found nothing out of the ordinary. When he was done, he radioed in the all-clear.

Jimmy made the same pattern of back-and-forth paths in the middle part of the island. He also observed nothing out of the ordinary. The all-clear for his sector was radioed in.

Zach made the back-and-forth pattern on the island's southern end. He saw nothing out of place in his watch area either. His all-clear radioed in and headed back to the Manor house. He was excited to see Samantha. They had made plans to go out to dinner on the mainland for their first date that evening.

They Face timed or texted every day since

she had given him her number. Zach had continued to see her every Thursday on his day off, but since she worked till late at night, they never had time to go out afterward. Nerves were setting in. Even though they knew everything about each other, Zach couldn't help but think she was way out of his league.

Samantha pulled up to the Manor house and found Zach sitting on his ATV, waiting for her. He slipped off his ATV, meeting her at her car. He pulled a bouquet from behind his back to give to her before opening the car door.

Amazed they weren't the standard roses most guys give women. Samantha smiled when she realized he had gotten her carnations instead. Her favorite flowers. This showed he listened when she talked. She reminisced about the conversation that contained that tid-bit of information.

She thanked him for the flowers, gave him a hug, and kissed him on the cheek. This made Zach blush. The way he blushed around her was such a charming quality to her.

Martin came out of the house and helped Zach carry Samantha's things up to the room she chose. Without letting her see what he was doing, Zach scanned the bedroom and ad-joining bathroom to ensure no surprises were waiting for her.

When he felt everything was clear, he re-laxed a bit more and started talking about his plans for their date.

"I get off work at 5:00 pm. So I will go home and change and pick you up around 5:30 pm

if that's okay with you? I have a pleasant night planned for us, Samantha. I hope you enjoy it."

"Sounds like you have put a lot of thought into all this. That is so sweet of you. I can't wait!"

Zach gave her a hug, kissed her forehead, and headed back to work. Samantha finished unpacking her things and then tried to pick the perfect outfit for their first date.

Jessica had heard Samantha had arrived and saw that Zach had left to go back to work. Jessica went to see her sister. Finding Samantha looking at several outfits laid out on her bed.

"Need some help there, little sis?"

"Yes! It's our first date. I want it to be exceptional and look good, but I want to be comfortable

too. I can't decide."

"Okay, okay. Breathe first. I like this green knit v-neck sweater. I think it will offset your red hair and bring out your green eyes. If you are going for comfort, wear these jeans. Oh, and wear these knee-high black boots. I think all of that will look great on you."

Samantha took the outfit Jessica chose and put it on. Then, looking in the full-length mirror, she turned side to side and smiled. Next, giving her big sister a big hug and a kiss on the cheek.

"It's perfect! Exactly what I was going for. Thank you so much."

The two girls sat on the bed and discussed their blooming relationships. They were like two schoolgirls sharing their innermost secrets. Jessica felt fortunate to have gotten to know her sister. It was as if they had known each other their entire lives. But she hated keeping the secret about the family's dangers from her. It was the best thing for now, though.

Zach was prompt. He was at the door at 5:29 pm, holding another bouquet and a box of chocolate. Martin let him in and called Samantha to let her know her date was here. Then, after some razzing by Richard Jr., David, Jimmy, and even Timothy, they set off for their date.

They took the rickety ferry to the mainland and drove to the Blue Parrot Mexican restaurant. He was enamoring Samantha with his efforts to make this a memorable date. Zach opened the car door for her and extended his hand, helping her out of the car. He held the restaurant door open for her and let her enter first.

Then he pulled her chair out for her and helped settle her in her seat before taking his. It was refreshing to be on a date with a polite gentleman. Even choosing her favorite type of food showed her he listened when she told him stuff about her.

They had a great time laughing and conversing as if they had known each other all their lives. Zach was becoming more and more comfortable around Samantha, and his shyness was disappearing. She could still make him blush, which she loved doing.

When the night was over, Zach dropped Samantha off at the front door of the Manor house. As they stood at the doorstep to say goodnight, Zach held both of Samantha's hands.

"May I give you a kiss goodnight?"

"Yes, I would love that."

Samantha looked into Zach's eyes. Zach leaned in and kissed her lips. Samantha felt the warmth in her cheeks, and she felt faint. The night had been flawless, with the perfect ending. Zach pulled away from the embrace looking in her eyes and sliding his hands out of hers to step away.

"Goodnight Samantha. Thank you for gracing me with your presence tonight."

"Goodnight Zach. Thank you for planning such and enchanting evening."

Samantha went up to her room to go to bed. Zach went home content in the thought the night went without fault. They both fell asleep thinking of love.

Samantha awoke to the sun, trying to shine through the slats of the blinds on her window. She rewound the memories of the night before over and over in her mind and smiled to herself. She had never had a more perfect night. Zach pulled her chair out for her, holding doors for her, making sure she was steady on her feet walking through the parking lot, charming her. The complete package she had always dreamed of. Spending so much time with him would be magical the next week.

She felt sad when she thought of going

back to Boston after the holidays. She didn't know if she could handle a long-distance relationship. Then she had a fabulous idea to move into the Manor house! Her brothers had already moved in. Things were going well for them and Jimmy. She didn't see why anyone would object to her moving in.

Samantha remembered Danielle was a waitress at the café on the mainland. She knew she could get a job working there. However, she needed to secure that before presenting the idea to Jessica, Jimmy, and her brothers. Motivated, she got up and took her shower. She got dressed and went downstairs for breakfast.

It surprised Samantha to see Danielle downstairs in the kitchen. She and Richard were sitting eating breakfast together at the kitchen island. While Samantha and Zach were out on their date, Richard and Danielle had their own. Catching up with them about their evening over breakfast, Samantha offered to take Danielle to work.

This gave Samantha the chance to talk to Danielle about getting a job at the café. Danielle was excited about the possibility of Samantha working with her and her living at the Manor house. It would be fun to have another girl around to hang out with when she visited Richard on the island. Since there was so much testosterone flowing in the house, it was sometimes overwhelming for her.

Danielle introduced Samantha to the manager at the café and then started her shift. They offered Samantha a job on the spot, and she told the manager she would let her know for sure the next day. Going back to the island, she was confident in her plan to move into the Manor house to spend more time with Zach.

While Samantha was out of the house, Jessica, Timothy, Jimmy, Richard Jr., David, and Zach had a quick meeting. They had made the appraisal that there wasn't any inclination that there would be a threat towards Samantha so far. However, Jessica and Timothy were taking turns checking her room to ensure there were no surprises left there for her. The lack of evidence of another deer's carcass so far led them all to believe there would be no heart left for Samantha.

Jessica let the others know what she and Timothy had found out about the symbolism of the heart being connected to dark magic or voodoo. Jimmy remembered hearing stories as a child about dark witches that had lived on the island many decades before. He could imagine no one on the island being into any of that.

David gave an update on the cameras he had ordered. The cameras would be in a few days after Christmas. They all agreed they would have to be even more vigilant about their security until then. They would scrutinize anything out of the ordinary.

He also told them how using the drone worked out well. In explaining how he used the drone, he also informed the others how close he could get to the herd of deer. They all found it fascinating. As they were finishing up their briefing, Samantha walked into the parlor.

"Hey everyone, glad you are all here. Especially you, Zach. I know I need to ask permission and make sure it's all okay with you all and dad, but I have decided that I want to move here to the island. I have already secured a waitressing job at the café on the mainland. So I guess it's up to you all and dad, of course."

As Samantha looked at everyone, Jessica's heart sank. She didn't want to say no to her sister. The smile on Samantha's face said it all. This was putting her in a dire predicament. If she said no, it would break her sister's heart. However, it could keep her safer. If she said yes, she might just put her sister in more harm's way. Looking at Jimmy, she could tell he had the same dilemma running through his head.

Zach just looked at Samantha and then

looked at the others. His heart was skipping beats. He wanted to see Samantha more regularly, yet he was terrified of losing her to some psychopath.

Richard Jr. ran his hands over his face in frustration. He was picking up that trait from his cousin. Then he shrugged his shoulders and looked at everyone else imploringly.

"We have to tell her. She needs to know what she is getting herself into."

"What do you need to tell me?"

Zach looked at Jimmy and motioned for him to tell her. Jimmy looked at Jessica, who looked back at him, defeated, and nodded her head. Then Jimmy informed Samantha about everything. It well enlightened her of the danger she was stepping into moving onto the island.

"Mom and Dad don't know about any of this?"

"Nope. Do you think they would have allowed David and me to remain on the island if they had known? They can't know. And if anything occurs while they are here, we need to all shrug it off as some stupid fraternity-type hazing incident. You understand."

"Got it. So I can move in then?"

Jimmy and Jessica both shrugged their shoulders and nodded yes. There was nothing they could do or say to change her mind. She hugged them both and then ran over to Zach and planted a big kiss on his lips in front of everyone. Zach turned the brightest shade of red.

"Alright guys, it's time to head out for work."

While the others went off to do their security details, Jessica, Timothy, and Samantha played pool in the parlor. Martin came and joined them since he had finished his work for the day and was waiting for Mira and Richard to arrive.

Chapter 14: Change of Plans

They were furious! Just when they were having fun torturing the family, the family had to fight back. The fact that the two Gardiner boys stuck it out and joined the security team irritated them. The younger Gardiner boys' ideas of cameras and drone use would cause a problem or two. This needed to be addressed.

The added security had made it harder to hunt for the more significant kills. This was causing them to be agitated. Their hatred for the family grew bigger daily. The fact they weren't scared off yet made them seethe.

They had the crows. It was close enough. They could start eliminating them one by one.

It would give them power and a way to relieve the stress and aggravation they were feeling.

The culling of the crows gave them great satisfaction. They decided on a unique method to extinguish the life force within the creature with each one.

The first one they took some bird seed and mixed it with Avitrol. The poison caused the bird to have violent convulsions until it died. The second bird they hit on the head with a hammer, rendering it lifeless. They started a fire in their fireplace and then proceeded to burn the third one alive. When it was time for the fourth one they drown it. The fifth and sixth were taken care of, one by slitting its throat and the other by piercing its heart.

As they did so, they imagined each bird

as a member of the Gardiner family until they were all lifeless. The rush of power had soothed the anger inside them, for now.

At least the listening devices in the house were coming in handy. They could hear all the new security plans, including potential round-the-clock bodyguards. This would be problematic in knocking them off one by one. The idea of eliminating them all at once crossed their mind again.

Nope, they knew that wouldn't work either. So they were going to have to back off a bit. To give the family a false sense of security would benefit them much more in the long run than keeping up the torture.

Dejected, since they couldn't torture Samantha like they had tortured the other siblings, they hatched a plan that would make up for it. The blossoming relationship between the young security guard Zach and the young Gardiner girl gave them more ideas. They knew their power would grow soon enough.

They had to have patience. The thoughts of how and when and who to eliminate first raced through their mind. They zeroed in on the who. Now they just needed to gather more information to figure out the how and when.

The timing was everything. They could not point fingers at themselves. It was imperative to their survival that all roads led to someone else, if at all. If things could look tragic, that would be best.

A few lives would be collateral damage. This fact didn't bother them one bit. It just meant more power to feed the darkness inside them.

They drew an upside-down pentagram on the wood floor and placed the lifeless bodies of the crows at the point of each triangle and one in the center. They added black candles and lit each one as they chanted an incantation. Each crow would hold a curse. The curses were to aid them in their mission against the family.

Their studies of dark magic had provided them with a wealth of knowledge. It was useful in their purpose against the family.

When they were done with their ritual, they prepared the family's gifts for Christmas. Then they blew out the candles, buried them in the backyard, and erased the pentagram off the floor.

Since they knew the family had connected the hearts to black magic or voodoo, they needed to be more careful. They should find no trace to tie them to any of what had occurred or what was to happen.

They had to stay one step ahead of the family at all times and at all costs. For their plan to succeed, no one could suspect them. They felt they were flying under the radar for the time being.

Samantha moving into the Manor house would make gathering information on her much more accessible. Yet again it was comical how much the family played right into their master plans. Unfortunately, they would be the reason for their own demise in the end.

The listening devices helped them listen

in on Jessica and Samantha's conversations, which already had proven to be helpful. Their bond was the strongest out of the siblings. That information would be beneficial. They could use that to hurt one or the other. Or even use it to break them both.

Both the girls were head over heels in love with their men. Their men seemed to reciprocate those feelings. However, they wondered if the seeds of doubt were planted, what would the outcome be.

They imagined the heartbreak they could cause, laughing. Messing with others' emotions had been a fun game they had learned long ago. They had even chased a few people off the island using those tactics. It was fun making people doubt their own emotions and their own sanity.

They wondered how long it would take poor Jimmy to go off the deep end again. Awareness of his weaknesses was so valuable. The most significant defect was his undying love for Melissa. She had left the island seven years ago and had yet to return. Consciousness about Jimmy and Melissa's chance encounter and the subsequent marriage proposal gave them a brilliant idea.

Arranging Melissa's need to come to the island would set Jimmy up for more heartache in the end. This would have to be fit into their plans somehow.

They needed to get back to work. If anyone noticed them gone, it would send up a red flag of suspicion. So they hid the presents and went back to work.

As they worked throughout the day, they gathered information. Using the knowledge, they continued to formulate their plans. Finally, they would take a break from torturing the family after Christmas. It would warn thoroughly the family of their fate. What the family did with that information would be interesting. The family would not escape the plans, but eventually, the entire family would be gone. Every one of them, even Jimmy.

Recognition from experiences in the past, the police would not be involved. The family liked to handle things on their own. They didn't know whether this was an ego thing or just a power trip. Either way, it played into their plans beautifully.

Chapter 15: Empty Nest

Mira and Richard pulled up to the Manor house just before dinnertime. The car behind them was Mira's parents. Martin came out to meet them all and to show them to their rooms. Jessica and Timothy greeted them also and helped with the grandparent's luggage.

By the time they were all in their rooms, it was time for dinner. Sitting down for dinner, Richard sat at the head of the table as he had years ago with Mary. It was a strange feeling sitting there with Mira and all of their children. A dream he had once had with Mary. To have family dinners nightly in this very dining room, as he had growing up.

Thoughts going back to his younger years, he was naïve to believe he and Mary would have lasted. They were so different in so many ways. He had loved the island and living there, but she loved it for the prestige it brought her, not like the connection he had.

While he wished they could have divorced amicably and avoided the tragic circumstances of their actions, he felt content with where his family was now. Richard missed his cousin Alexandria and her family. The memories of his childhood were vivid in this house. That guilt he carried with him daily. As he sat there in the Manor house those feelings filled him with more remorse.

Mira was beaming with happiness. She had missed her boys and was still adjusting to their decision to move to the island. At least Samantha was still living at home with her and Richard. It was nice to be eating dinner together as a family again.

Mira had never felt comfortable on the island, especially knowing she was of a different social class than Richard had been. Although her parents acted pretentious as if they were the same, they felt like they and their daughter belonged on the island. Her parents sat at the dinner table pretending as if they had belonged there their entire lives.

The conversation flowed from discussing who would attend the Christmas Eve open house the next night, to how the wedding plans were going. Jessica bristled at the many questions about the wedding and the onslaught of suggestions from her grandmother. Timothy sensed her feelings of tension.

"Jessica, you haven't told them the main course is going to be crocodile stew yet?"

Jessica almost choked on the mouthful of food she was chewing and nudged him with her leg. All except her Grandparents found the suggestion amusing. Jimmy and the others followed Timothy's lead and started suggesting the most outrageous foods they could think of.

"I vote for Rocky Mountain oysters."

Becoming a sort of game with them all. Even her parents chimed in.

"Your mother and I suggest Fried Silkworm."

The grandparents didn't see the humor in any of it. Instead, they grumbled and commented on how uncivilized today's youth were.

When dinner was over, they all retired into the parlor. Jessica's grandparents hadn't been to the Manor house in many, many years and were not at all impressed with the changes Jimmy had made to the parlor. Their comments were it made it look like commoners lived there. Jessica and her siblings rolled their eyes at each other. Jimmy shrugged off the comments.

Zach stopped by to visit Samantha and became inundated with questions from her parents and grandparents. They were like piranhas on a piece of meat. Now Jessica understood why Samantha wanted to move out. But, thinking about that, Jessica wondered when Samantha would spring that revelation on her parents. Then as if Samantha had read Jessica's mind she started the conversation.

"Hey, Mom, Dad, I have some really great news. I got a new job working with Danielle at that little café on the mainland. I want to move in here with Jimmy, Richard, and David. It's all okay with them, as long as it is okay with you guys. Isn't that great?"

Richard looked at his youngest daughter and then looked at his wife. Mira had tears welling up in her eyes. She knew someday she would have an empty nest. She just never expected it to be so soon and so sudden. They had just become a whole family again, finding Jessica. Mira was not ready for all her children to fly on their own. He put his arm around his wife to comfort her.

"Is this because of this young man?"

"Partially, Dad, I have been saving up to move out on my own for a while now. But, yes, I want to be closer to Zach. It's not like I will live by myself. I got these guys to keep me safe and out of trouble."

"Your mind is set? Just know if it doesn't work out, you can always come back home."

Samantha gave both of her parents a big hug.

The grandparents thought it was a crazy idea. They didn't understand the rush of the youth of the day to move out and be on their own. Finally, they were tired and said good-night to everyone else and went to bed. Soon after, Mira and Richard retired to their bedroom.

Everyone else stayed up playing pool and drinking beer. Jimmy had one and only one. That morning was the first in a while he hadn't woken up with beer cans strewn all over his floor. The irony of not discovering a deer carcass or deer's heart wasn't lost on him with the absence of the beer cans. He wanted to make sure none of those things returned, so he was diligent about only drinking the one.

The next day would be hectic, and he wanted to make sure he was at his best mentally. However, the planning he had done for weeks for the Christmas Eve open house would hopefully go smoothly. His only concern was that security would be not as tight as usual since they had invited all team members to attend.

The security team all had agreed to treat it as an undercover type assignment and take turns patrolling outside so everyone could enjoy themselves. Jimmy had already vowed to himself he would not have a drop of alcohol, just to be sure he stayed alert.

He turned in earlier than the others. Although his body ached with exasperation, sleep eluded him for the first few hours. Anxiety filled his mind. The party would be the first big event on the island in years. Success, or failure, depended on so many things. Keeping everyone safe was the number one priority. The only problem he had was figuring out who he was trying to keep everyone safe from.

The nagging in the back of his mind whether he could be the one doing the tormenting scared him. He loved his cousins and would never knowingly or consciously want to hurt them. Although it was his subconscious, he was concerned with. That part of himself that he knew could lose touch with reality.

Seven years was a long time, though, to go without an episode. Could the events of the last few months have triggered something in himself? He hadn't talked to his therapist in three years. The need to continue therapy wasn't there, and even she had agreed he was doing so well. Maybe it was time to resume.

Even though Mira and Richard had gone to bed hours before their children, they had lain awake discussing the turn of events. Shocked that all three of their children had decided to move to the island, they were trying to come to grips with it all.

Both were not fully accepting of their children's decisions. Mira was having a hard time thinking she would come home to an empty house from now on. Her heart hurt. As a mother, she knew her children were supposed to move on with their lives. She just didn't want it to be now.

Richard understood the allure of the island. He had grown up there. But, although he had wanted to raise his family there, fate had seen fit to ensure that did not happen. Or, more appropriately, Mary had been determined to ensure that did not happen.

As he held Mira in his arms and discussed their feelings on the matter, Richard could not help but feel a bit of remorse at how they had handled Mary and Benjamin's plot.

Maybe he should have gone to the authorities with the plot to kill him. Would they have believed him, anyway? He had regrets. His actions had caused the death of his cousin's family. That was something he could never forgive himself for.

Their children were good-hearted people. They were just ready to spread their wings sooner than either of them wanted to acknowledge. Richard pitched the idea of Mira and him moving into the Manor house as well. Mira couldn't. The idea of living in the same place that his ex-wife was willing to kill for creeped her out.

Staying at the house for even a few days was difficult for her. There were times she felt every portrait on the walls watching her every move. She even thought she could hear whispering about her as she walked the halls. If you let it, one's imagination could also convince one of the nefarious things. Mira's imagination did just that in the Manor house. They eventually could fall asleep.

Jessica and Timothy said goodnight to her siblings. They went to their room and got ready for bed. Laying in Timothy's arms, Jessica let the tension of the day slip away. He kissed her forehead and dropped asleep. Jessica found her own eyes heavy with sleep and followed suit.

Richard Jr. and Danielle had retreated to his room for the night. She was spending more and more time at the Manor house. This was the second night she had felt too tired to make

Richard Jr. drive her home. He was more than happy to share his bed with her, in all honesty.

They hadn't yet actually made love to one another. Richard felt that the time would be soon to take that next step in their relationship. Sleeping with her in his arms, though, made restraining himself difficult. He didn't want to push it. She was his best friend, and if something went horribly wrong and they broke up, it would devastate him to lose her. They fell asleep rather quickly, tranquil in each other's arms.

Samantha and Zach were the last ones awake.

"I can't believe you are moving to the island. Like, don't get me wrong I am happy about it. I just never thought you would really be into me, let

alone want to move here. Most mainlanders have no desire to live here."

"Well, I am not just any mainlander. It is my birthright to live here, so why not claim that, right? And being near you is a big bonus."

Zach held one of Samantha's hands while sitting with his arm around her. She leaned her head on his shoulder. The scent of her hair smelled of lilacs, and he let go of her hand to sweep a strand of hair out of her eyes.

Samantha had never dated a guy as sweet as Zach. Most of the men she dated in the past were looking for a quick fling. Something she utterly despised. They made her feel like a slab of meat at a market. Zach was so different.

His touch was always so careful and gentle, as if she was fragile like fine china, and he didn't want to break her. This was so adorable to her and was one thing she loved most about him. The way he actually listened to her talk. And how he remembered what she had said in previous conversations were other traits that just made her fall in love with him.

It was late, and although Zach didn't live far from the Manor house, Samantha convinced him to stay the night with her.

"It's late. You are tired. Come upstairs and sleep in my room," Samantha said while getting off the sofa and pulling Zach with her.

"Samantha, there is something you should know," Zach said, standing firm where he was.

"What's that?"

"I never have... what I mean... I'm a virgin."

"Yeah, so? I am too. We don't have to have sex if we sleep together. When we are both ready, when the time is right, if it's right, then we can take that next step."

Zach smiled and blushed while letting Samantha lead the way to her bedroom. He was nervous about sharing a bed with her.

The first time he had seen her, he had known he wanted her in the worst way, at Alexandria's funeral. That desire had fueled his trips to Boston to eat dinner at the restaurant she worked at. Then, it fueled him to ask her for her number despite feeling she was way out of his league.

Now, knowing she was also a virgin just made him want her more. He wanted their first time to be absolutely special. That would take some planning and a lot of self-control. The self-control part would be the hardest. Making sure he didn't go too far too soon. Just the thought of being with her intimately someday aroused him.

At the doorway to her bedroom, she paused. Samantha looked at him and smiled while turning the doorknob. Then she led him in and closed the door behind them. Samantha could tell he was nervous. What he didn't know was she was just as scared.

Sharing a bed with a man was something she had never done before. Appreciation that he was a virgin too, eased her mind. There were no expectations between them and no one to compare her to. She didn't know if he expected anything to happen, but she didn't want to rush into anything.

Samantha grabbed a t-shirt and sweat-pants from her bureau, going to the bathroom to change.

Zach sat on the edge of the bed. While taking his shirt off and contemplating whether he should sleep in his pants.

When Samantha came out of the bathroom and saw Zach without his shirt, she felt the heat in her cheeks rise.

The sight of his chest, along with his chiseled abdomen, tempted her to run her hands over his bare skin. Instead, biting her lip, she averted her eyes from him and concentrated on the lamp on her bedside table.

This might be more difficult than she

thought. The view of Zach sitting on the edge of her bed, looking completely vulnerable yet absolutely gorgeous, made her want him. Trying to keep her composure.

"You can make yourself comfortable. I have two brothers. I have seen guys in their underwear before. So if you want to sleep in your underwear, feel free."

He took in Samantha, walking out of the bathroom as she put her hair up in a bun. Zach could see the outline of her body through her white t-shirt. This was not helping him keep himself in check.

He noticed her cheeks flush when she saw him sitting shirtless. Which also was not keeping him from feeling as if he wanted to do more than just sleep with her. When she told him he could sleep in his underwear, he thought he might lose control. How could he expect to sleep next to her, almost wholly naked, feeling nothing at all?

With a bit of trepidation, Samantha slid under the covers of her bed.

He struggled to hide his nerves. Zach went to the opposite side, slipped his pants off, and quickly slipped under the covers. It was awkward for both of them. They both felt the desire inside them. Yet, they were both trying not to act on it. Finally, Zach rolled over to face Samantha and kissed her forehead.

"Goodnight Sam, is it okay if I call you Sam?"

"Goodnight. You can call me anything you want, dear."

Samantha leaned over and kissed Zach softly on the lips. Tasting her soft rose-colored lips on his did him in. He pulled her towards him and kissed her back, longingly and deeply. Then, Reciprocating, she explored his body with her hands.

"I want you," he said.

"I want you too."

"Now?"

"Yes."

"Are you sure?"

"Yes."

"I love you, Sam."

"I love you too, Zach."

Chapter 16: Preparations

In the morning, Jimmy was the first to awake. As he swung his legs out from under his covers and onto the floor, it thrilled him to find no traces of any beer cans. He breathed a sigh of relief.

There was much to do, so he quickly showered and got dressed. Stella was already busy in the kitchen preparing the family their morning breakfast. He ate his breakfast, drank his coffee, and then reminded her she had off in the afternoon and evening. The caterers would be here at noontime to prepare for the party.

As he finished up his coffee, a van pulled

into the driveway. He went out and met with the driver and his passenger. They were the party decorators. Then another van with a trailer came up behind them. It was the tent he rented to be set up in the gardens. Jimmy showed them where everything was supposed to go, and they set out to get it all set up.

Next on his agenda, morning rounds, and heading to the security shack. He was always the first one to come and relieve the night crew. Those who had worked overnight usually filled him in on any unusual occurrences, which there had been none. The day shift crew was trickling in.

At the Manor house, Zach woke up to his phone alarm going off. He fumbled around to grab his phone out of his pants pocket on the floor. The beeping silenced, Zach turned to see if it had woken up Samantha. He felt horrible when he realized it had. He leaned over and kissed her on the forehead.

"I am sorry, didn't mean to wake you. I hate to leave, but I have to get to work. Thank you for last night. I love you more than anything."

"It's okay. I need to get up and get ready for the day, anyway. I wish you could stay, but I understand. Thank you for last night. I love you too. I will see you tonight, right? At the party."

"Yes, I will be here for the party. See you tonight."

As they finished their conversation, Zach threw on his clothes from the night before. He knew he didn't have time to run home and shower and change. So he, in haste, made his way downstairs and through the kitchen. He grabbed a freshly baked cranberry muffin Stella had cooled on a rack and a quick cup of coffee and headed out the door.

Stella raised her eyebrows at seeing him in her kitchen and smiled.

Zach made it to the security shack before Richard Jr. and David. He full tilt went to his locker, where he always had an extra pair of clothes, and grabbed them. Zach switched clothes in the bathroom and stashed his dirty clothes in his locker before either of Samantha's brothers made it into work.

He was hoping they hadn't seen him leave their sister's bedroom or the Manor house. That was a confrontation and conversation he did not want to have.

Jimmy had seen Zach come in through the doorway of his office and watched him go wild, changing so no one would realize he spent the night with Samantha. He thought it was pretty comical and debated whether to have some fun at Zach's expense or not. Deciding to forego having fun, he figured he would keep Zach's secret for now.

Richard Jr. left Danielle sleeping soundly in his bed. He wrote her a sweet note telling her he would see her later at the party. He watched her sleep in his bed peacefully, making him want to crawl back into bed and snuggle up to her. But that would be a mistake because then he would be late for work. So, he made it down to the kitchen for breakfast before David and figured he would meet him at the shack.

David got up and headed downstairs for breakfast. He loved Stella's cooking and always looked forward to having an excellent, warm breakfast before heading off to work.

His mom was never big on cooking, so it was something he loved about living on the island. In addition, Stella was always so friendly to him, which made the mornings much more enjoyable. There were no expectations from her and no judgments.

"Stella, thank you for always making such delicious breakfasts. They really help me start my day off."

"You are welcome. It's my job to make sure everyone in the house eats. Even the stragglers."

"Stragglers?"

"Yeah, you don't have any yet, but it seems each of your siblings has one."

"Oh, you mean boyfriends or girlfriends. Yeah, I don't have one of those yet. Not sure I will have one anytime soon."

"Why not? You are a handsome young man. I am sure the ladies adore you."

"Well, the ladies adore me. I am just not sure I adore them."

"Oh. Regardless of who adores you or who you adore, you will find your soul mate someday. You will see."

"See, that's the problem, Stella, and I haven't ever uttered these words out loud to anybody before. I am physically attracted to women. Yet my soul finds a connection with men. It's so confus-

ing. I don't know if I will ever find the one."

"Oh, dear boy. That does sound confusing and burdensome. Just try to stay true to yourself, and whatever comes will be. It will all work itself out. Take your time to find out who you really are and what you really want. Then the rest will fall into place."

"Thanks, Stella."

Soon the day crew was all at the shack, including David. They had their morning briefing before heading out on their various patrols. Jimmy sensed most of the staff were excited about the party later and really not focusing as they usually did. So he headed out on patrol, stopping at the Manor house to check on the preparations for the party. Everything was going as planned.

There was excitement in the air among everyone on the island. While the family awoke and made their way downstairs for breakfast. There was a bustle of activity outside the Manor house and even inside. The professional decorators made sure the place was festive looking inside and out.

Jessica noticed her sister, Samantha, had an extra bounce in her step. This she attributed to her sister moving onto the island. She felt thrilled for her. It was lovely watching her siblings spread their wings. She had been on her own for a few years now, so observing them change as their lives evolved was interesting.

They had all had the shock of learning about their parent's pasts a few months prior, and Jessica couldn't help but think that learning the truth had shaped all of their futures. It seemed to have jump-started them all into making some significant changes in their lives for her siblings. All of them moving away from their parents was a noteworthy change. A change she was curious to see how her parents would genuinely handle.

Danielle soon arrived down in the kitchen and realized she needed a ride home since Richard Jr. was working.

"I can bring you home. Just let me get my keys."

Samantha offered to bring her there.

"Do you two mind if I tag along? I really don't want to be stuck here with mom and dad and the grandparents. Timothy is still sleeping."

Danielle and Samantha both agreed. Once they were all in the car, Samantha spilled the beans about Zach spending the night.

"Oh my god, guys, I have been dying to tell somebody all morning! Zach and I slept together last night!"

"Wait, did you sleep together, or did you SLEEP together?"

Danielle Felt jealous that Samantha and Zach might have gotten more consequential than she and Richard had gotten.

"Woah, little sis. I hope you aren't rushing into this too fast."

"Well, we didn't intend to do anything but sleep. Since we were both virgins and all, we wanted the first time to be special."

"WERE virgins. That means you two did more than just sleep! So, how was it?"

The jealousy was hard to suppress for Danielle.

"So WAS it special?"

Jessica was concerned at the fast course their relationship was taking.

"Yes! It was magical in every way! I mean, I don't know how it was supposed to feel, but that's how it felt to me. But, of course, I have nothing to compare it to being a virgin and all. He was so gentle. It was the best early Christmas present I have ever received!"

Danielle was happy for Samantha that her first experience with Zach was good. Jealousy was flowing through her a bit, though, since she and Richard had been dating for far longer.

Then Danielle thought about how long it took for Richard to first kiss her. She had started to have feelings for him long before he had feelings for her, or at least long before he showed those feelings.

If they were going to move to the next level of their relationship, she felt she would have to make the first move. As she got out of Samantha's car and said goodbye, her thoughts went to when she would make her move on Richard. After the party, later tonight would be perfect.

Jessica couldn't believe her little sister was talking to her about having sex for the first time. It felt awkward at first. But then, she appreciated the fact her sister felt comfortable enough sharing private information with her. It was a testament to the unbreakable bond that had formed so quickly between them.

She remembered the first time she and Timothy had made love. Smiling to herself, she realized she couldn't be so critical of her sister. She and Timothy had known each other far less than Samantha and Zach.

They got back to the Manor house around the same time the caterers arrived. The place was still bustling with preparations for the party. Arthur had come while the girls were gone, and with him, he had brought Allison.

Jessica was happy to see them both. She knew Arthur had been having a hard time after the death of Alexandria, and she felt being around the family would help him. Jessica hoped to piece together more clues with Allison and her possible relationship with Timothy.

Timothy, Arthur, and Allison were in the parlor chatting when Jessica walked in. It seemed that Timothy and Allison had hit it off and were engaged in conversation. So she sat across from them and observed and listened to them both. The first thing she noticed was they both had green eyes. The shape was contrasting, but the color was the same.

Their conversation paused, and they both looked at Jessica. As they did, she noticed their jawlines were similar. Both of them had the same shaped nose as well. Jessica believed in her heart that they somehow were related.

"Don't let me interrupt."

Timothy smiled at her and turned back to the conversation he was having with Allison. Allison seemed genuinely interested in Timothy and his life. Especially his work as a writer. A slight twinge of jealousy ran through Jessica's mind. Then she reeled those thoughts in quickly. She knew Timothy had no romantic interest in Allison. She also felt Allison knew she was old enough to be his mother.

The irony of that last thought struck her instantly. Holding in all her questions for Allison was becoming increasingly more complex. Knowing she had to tread lightly with her, though, was what kept her from unleashing her inquiries.

Arthur started a conversation with Jessica and drew her attention away from Timothy and Allison. She welcomed the reprieve.

"How are the wedding plans going, Jessica?"

"They are coming along. I picked my dress. Samantha did a great job of helping me. Since fashion is not my thing."

Richard and Mira joined everyone in the parlor as they had come back from doing some last-minute gift buying on the mainland. Mira joined the conversation between Arthur and Jessica.

"She chose the most beautiful dress."

"I know Alexandria would have loved to be a part of that."

Jessica reached over and squeezed Arthur's hand. He appreciated the sentiment.

Everyone decided it would be wise to get ready for the evening's festivities late in the afternoon. Betty showed Allison where she could freshen up and change into the outfit she had brought.

Before Timothy and Jessica headed to their room, Martin brought another guest into the parlor. It was Jack, Timothy's cousin. Jessica welcomed him and then excused herself to go get ready. Timothy showed Jack up to a room where he could use to get changed for the party.

"I am so glad you could join us."

"I wouldn't miss this for the world. I can't believe I am here. On Gardiners Island, with my cousin."

Chapter 17: The Party

Jimmy had gotten off from work and dressed in a formal suit for the party. He felt out of place since he lived in his work clothes ninety percent of the time.

The Gardiners had thrown lavish parties, though, and he wanted to live up to that reputation. With a bit of a twist, though. Those who worked on the island usually performed their duties at these events. But not this time. He made sure everyone on the island who worked or lived there received invitations and was welcome. Purely as guests not employees.

This had indeed improved morale on the island for the few weeks leading up to the party. Jimmy had hired all outside help for the evening. He wanted everyone who attended to enjoy themselves as much as possible.

He was the first to be ready and stood in the entranceway, prepared to greet guests as they arrived. People showed up at 5 o'clock on the dot. The first few guests were some inhabitants of the island. They all seemed beyond a doubt excited to be included on the guest list. Some families from the mainland also arrived.

The great room on the Southern end of the house served as the prominent gathering place for the party. The French doors opened up to the gardens, covered by the party tent. They dispersed propane heaters throughout the tent area to give guests warmth.

Knocking on her door, Jessica checked on

Allison to show her down to the party. Before going to the door Allison smoothed the skirt she was wearing and nervously gave herself a once over in the mirror, then opened the door.

"Everything okay?"

"Yeah, I just get nervous in new surroundings. I am not one for enormous crowds and such."

"Stick with me. I am still new to all of this, too. But we will get through it together, okay?"

Jessica locked her elbow around Allison's elbow smiling.

"Thank you. Being a grown woman and not feeling comfortable in large gatherings, I feel silly. Having an ally helps."

"No worries. Let's go have some fun."

The two women went downstairs and into the great room together. Jessica spotted Timothy and Jack over in a corner, talking. Jack's back was to them as they walked up to the pair.

As Allison recognized Jack, she froze. She couldn't fathom why her cousin's son had an invitation to the party. Jack turned just as she froze. He took a sip of his drink, stopping when he saw his cousin's reaction to him being there. Then, making quick work of the distance between them, he walked up to Jessica and Allison.

"Hey cuz, fancy meeting you here. I see you look shocked at my presence."

Jack gave Allison a hug. She reluctantly reciprocated. Then stepped back.

"Well, yeah. This party is for the Gardiner family, friends, and employees. So, how the heck did you get an invitation?"

"I can answer that," Timothy said. "Jack and I just of late connected through a genealogy website. We are second cousins. He is the only biological family connection I have so, Jessica and I invited him."

"Oh. Jack, is he related to you through your father's side or your mother's side?" Allison had some trepidation in her voice.

"We don't know, but my mom sent in her DNA to either confirm or deny whether it relates him through her side or my dad's. Seeing we don't know about my dad or his side of the family, it's the easiest way to help narrow down the search."

"Ah. I see. Well, I hope you all figure it out.

I am parched, so I am going to find myself some-thing to drink at the moment."

They watched her walk away, and Jessica looked at Jack and Timothy with raised eye-brows.

"That was strange. For someone who was just terrified of coming down her by herself not more than five minutes ago, she sure got over that quickly."

"That's my cousin for you. She has always been an odd duck in social situations. Although, I think seeing me here was a big surprise."

"Yeah she surely had no expectation of any-one other than Arthur being here that she knows. I still think there is a connection between her and Timothy. I see similarities in your facial features."

"I agree. Talking with her earlier, I noticed some things that gives me a feeling of relatedness."

"I see it too, cuz."

"I think its best we don't push the conversation with her though any further until we get the results back from Jack's mom. We don't want to put her in a precarious position if she is not related."

"Oh absolutely."

The rest of the guests were mingling along with the family members. Lena and her family had arrived and were busy catching up with Mira and Richard. Even Lena's mom Rita had tagged along since her husband Tom was on a business trip and would be home first thing in the morning.

Everyone seemed to have a great time. Samantha was hanging out with Zach and his parents. Jessica noticed how Samantha and Zach were holding hands. She thought it was so sweet-looking. She wondered if she and Timothy gave off that same glowing aura of love and happiness when they were side by side.

There was less public display of affection between her brother Richard and Danielle. Although you could see their mannerisms and how they looked at each other, they were indeed in love. Then there was David. He seemed lost in the sea of people.

Jessica saw the uneasiness in his stance. His hands were in his pockets and then out of his pockets. He shifted his weight from one leg to the other. Danielle's sisters, Stephanie and

Erica, seemed to keep engaging him in conversation or even getting him out on the dance floor. Yet, he showed no genuine interest in them. Observing her little brother, she sensed his awkwardness around the two women who seemed enamored by him.

What was refreshing to see was the workers from the island interacting with everyone and having a great time. Watching Samuel and Betty both at the bar, impressing Jessica at how elegant they both looked. Samuel was wearing a nice suit, and Betty wore a red cocktail dress. The scooped neck of her dress added some dimension to her tall, skinny figure. Neither of them stayed at the bar for long. Jessica watched as David walked up to the bartender.

"Can I have a beer, please?"

"Can I see your ID, please?"

"Sorry, I don't have it on me at the moment. I am David Gardiner, though. I live here."

"Oh, my apologies, sir."

The bartender handed David the beer, and David thanked him. Then, standing next to the bar, David made quick work of the first beer and asked for another one.

"Easy there. You may want to slow down some, man."

"I know, I know. I just need something to calm my nerves and all."

"What's got you all in knots?"

"People. I just feel so alone, even in this sizeable crowd."

"You? Alone? Dude, you have so much going for you. You are handsome. You are rich. And you have several beautiful young women following you around tonight."

"Yes, even with all that going for me, I feel alone. But wait, how do you know about the women following me?"

"Um, well, I noticed you right away. As I said, you are handsome. So I was watching you. I hope you don't mind?"

David didn't mind. He found it comforting that he stood out to someone out of all these people. It didn't bother him that the bartender was another man.

He stood at the bar most of the evening, getting to know the bartender, named Joe. Stephanie and Erica came up, trying to get

David to leave his post and go dance with them. They succeeded once, although he headed back to the bar when the song was over.

Jessica noticed the difference in David as he stayed at the bar talking with the bartender. She didn't know whether it was the alcohol he was consuming or the potential friendship he was making. The reason didn't matter. What mattered was her brother's happiness.

Jimmy was mingling with everyone and having a great time. He felt the event was an immense success. Cracking open a beer and toasting with David for a great night. In the back of his mind, though, he was determined to only have the one beer.

As the evening got later, guests left. Arthur and Allison said their goodbyes and thanked the family for the invite, then headed on their way home. The stragglers were the family, some workers, and Lena's family.

Rita was at the bar next to Samuel. Samuel recognized her from the wedding he had attended with Mary many years ago. He thought that night would have started a beautiful relationship with Mary. She wasn't interested in having a relationship with a lowly mechanic, though. She just used him for her needs and cast him aside.

When Mary had gotten drunk, she would go to his place and get what she wanted from him. He supposed her way of thanking him was leaving him a sizeable amount of money in her will. Seeing Rita again brought back memories of how flirtatious she had been with him that night. Striking up a conversation with her, he hoped she would be just as flirtatious.

"Remember me, darling?"

Rita remembered Samuel. His allure attracted her to him at her daughter's wedding. Although, she realized a lot of the enticement towards him was that he had accompanied her cousin Mary to the wedding. Her husband was away on business, making it a straightforward decision for her to go along with his flirting and see where it led. Her marriage had been all but dead for several years now. They stayed together because it was the easiest thing to do.

When Lena was ready to leave, she couldn't find her mother anywhere. Calling her cell phone, she located her. Within minutes Rita appeared, coming down the stairs. She told her daughter the downstairs bathroom was being used, so she had found one upstairs to use.

Jack left after Lena's family, and Timothy and Jessica headed upstairs to their room. It surprised them to meet Samuel in the hallway leading towards the stairs. As he walked past them, he grumbled something about having to use the bathroom.

When they got to their room, they found a gift addressed to Jessica with instructions not to open until the following day. The hair raised on the back of her neck. Timothy didn't like the looks of this gift. They knew the rest of the family was still downstairs, so they made haste to everyone's rooms. Just as they suspected, there was a gift for each family member. They gathered them all up and brought them to their room.

They did not want to ruin everyone's festive mood. So Jessica and Timothy hid the gifts in the bathroom closet and did not tell anyone else about them. Thinking that tomorrow morning after they had opened up all their presents, something would be said if the surprises were from someone in the family. In that case, they would bring the gifts to everyone. If no one mentioned them, they would let Jimmy know and investigate further.

The last guest left late in the evening, and Jimmy supervised the clean-up. The decorators would leave the decorations up for a couple of days and also the tent. After that, it would be easier to take it all down during daylight hours.

Earlier, much to Danielle's dismay, when her mother and father left, they insisted she go home with them. So Richard Jr. went to bed alone, and her plans to take their relationship to the next level were foiled.

Samantha and Zach had waited until everyone else had gone up to their rooms, except Jimmy. Then they snuck up to her room to be alone for a bit before Zach went home for the evening.

David had enjoyed hanging out with Joe. They had struck up a friendship. So they made plans to hang out on their next day off. David didn't know where the fellowship would go. He just knew they seemed to hit it off.

By the time Jimmy had finished up, the entire house was quiet. Everything had gone off without a hitch. He felt a bit more relaxed that whoever had been tormenting the family had stopped. It was a peaceful Christmas Eve, and as he looked out the window, he noticed snow falling.

It was beautiful to see it come down. There was a tranquility that seemed to envelop the house. Jimmy could only pray that the following morning would be just as serene. He went to bed the most relaxed he had been in days. Soon he was off to dreamland, where his mind went to Melissa and his true heart's desire.

Chapter 18: Christmas Morning

Stella was up early and over at the Manor house, making a big Christmas breakfast for the family. It comprised of eggs, bacon, sausage, chocolate chip pancakes, regular pancakes, French toast, and waffles. The aromas wafted up to the second floor and aroused the house's occupants out of their slumbers.

As they awakened, one by one, they made their way down into the dining room, where Stella had arranged chaffing dishes on the sidebar. Each person served themselves and sat at the table, eating the delectable foods Stella had prepared.

Before Jessica and Timothy went downstairs, they ensured the gifts they had found were secure in the closet from the night before. They were there all right, and Jessica couldn't help but have an ominous feeling about them. Praying she was wrong, they had gone down to breakfast with the family.

Jimmy was one of the last ones to arise. As he slid his feet onto the floor, it horrified him to find empty beer cans strewn over his bedroom floor. He knew he had only one beer all night, or that is what he could remember. Panic filled him with what awaited for the day. He had come to realize that the beer cans coincided with ominous events.

Joining the family downstairs for breakfast, he scanned faces to see if anyone seemed alarmed or distressed. Everyone seemed joyous and content eating the fabulous breakfast his mother had prepared for them all. He saw nothing unusual in any of their faces.

The family had their fill to eat by mid-morning and settled into the parlor to exchange gifts. They were all excited to see how their loved ones liked the presents they had picked out for one another.

Jessica opened her gift from Jimmy first. When she opened it and realized he had gotten her a bunch of different filters for her camera, she became misty-eyed. The last time anyone had bought her a Christmas gift that had to do with photography was the last Christmas with her adoptive dad. So getting the thoughtful gift from Jimmy meant the world to her.

"Jimmy, holy cow, thank you! These will get

used tremendously."

Next, Samantha opened her gift from Jessica. It was a snow globe with two girls holding hands. A ribbon on the front said, *Having a Sister Means Having A Friend Forever.* Samantha was in love with the gift by Jessica, giving her a hug and saying thank you. Carefully, she wrapped it back in the tissue paper and placed it in the box, so it would not get ruined before she could bring it up to her room.

Jimmy had gotten both the boys a crossbow to learn to hunt with. He also had paid for hunting courses for them to take. Both of them thought it was the most incredible gift ever. They couldn't wait to learn how to shoot the crossbows. But when they lifted them up and acted as if they would shoot them, it was distressing to their grandparents.

"Be careful. You might accidentally hurt some-one with those."

"Grandpa, they aren't even loaded with arrows."

David shrugged his shoulders as Richard Jr. admonished his Grandfather.

Grandma and Grandpa Kennedy had got-ten the girls a cardigan sweater, a Michael Kors handbag, and diamond earrings with a pen-dant necklace. In addition, they had bought the boys each a cardigan sweater, men's Michael Kors wallet, and a Rolex watch. Materialistic items that were not unique or personal for any of them. The gifts were impractical for them all in their careers. Their grandparents did not understand the lives they lived.

Mira and Richard had gotten each of their kids a picture frame that said *family*. They requested they get a family portrait done while they were all together during the week. It was a sweet, sentimental gift for them all, which had more meaning now that they were all not living at home. Jessica told them she could easily set her equipment up to take a timed picture. They had gotten them many other items that weren't highly extraordinary.

Richard Jr. and David had taken the easy way out and bought everyone gift cards. Everyone laughed because they did simple gifts.

However, they had wrapped them in the most creative and challenging ways. They had covered the gift card in a box for Jimmy with several other packages. The boys wrapped each one in a complicated manner to be unwrapped. They covered one in duct tape, while they covered another in zip ties.

The family all laughed at the creativity and the challenges. The boys had sent Jessica and Samantha on a scavenger hunt for theirs, with envelopes containing clues.

Jessica had gotten her brothers hunting knives and some rugged work boots, which they both appreciated. Living on the island, both would get used. She also got Jimmy a hunting knife and had the blade engraved with the initials JG. He enjoyed the sentiment and knew his cousin wanted him to know she acknowledged he was family, even though they couldn't publicly.

Samantha had gone for the fun gifts and

got everyone a different version of the game, *Cards Against Humanity.* They were all looking forward to playing later that night.

Timothy opened the present from Jessica. It blew him away by the sentimentalism. It was pictures of him and her and various places they had been together so far in their relationship. He gave her a hug and kiss and told her how much he loved the gift and her. Then he handed her his gift to her.

The box was wrapped in green shiny paper with a curly bow. She carefully unwrapped it, and opened the box. Inside was a custom-made snow globe with a replica of her log cabin. It was quickly her favorite gift.

The siblings had bought their mother and grandmother a mother's ring and a grandmother's ring with their birthstones. Then, since both their father and grandfather loved golf, they had pitched in and bought them both membership at the local country club.

They finished opening gifts by mid-afternoon, and nobody mentioned the presents that remained unopened in Jessica's bathroom closet, the ones found in each of the family's rooms. Finally, Richard Jr. excused himself to go spend some time with Danielle. Grandma and Grandpa Kennedy headed back home to Connecticut, and Samantha headed to Zach's to spend some time with him and his family.

Jimmy excused himself also to go spend some time with his parents. Jessica debated whether she should tell Jimmy about the gifts sitting upstairs. Then, deciding it could wait until he got back from seeing his parents, she kept quiet.

By dinnertime, everyone had gathered back at the house. Danielle had come back with Richard Jr., and Zach had come back with Samantha. After dinner, they gathered to play pool and some *Cards Against Humanity.* Laughter by all filled the evening. It genuinely was a Merry Christmas. After the chaos and heartache, the family had endured the past few months. It was calming to have some normalcy.

Once Mira and Richard went to bed, though, Jessica knew she and Timothy had to tell the others about the random gifts left for each of them.

"Guys, I hate to ruin the night. But Timothy and I found presents for the family in our rooms

last night. We waited all day because we didn't know who they were from. Since no one has piped up, we assume, our fiendish friend left them. They are upstairs in my bathroom closet."

Jimmy went upstairs with Timothy and Jessica to retrieve the presents. His gut was twisting and turning. He thought they had made it through two whole days with no incidents from the unknown predator. The only thing that bothered him was the beer cans no one else knew about.

"Are you sure these gifts aren't by anyone else?"

"Jimmy, there is no indication who they are from on the packages. And no one has mentioned them all day. I think it's safe to say that they aren't from anyone here."

They brought the packages downstairs. No one recognized them. Not knowing what the contents might be they agreed it would be safer to open them at the security shack. They all bundled up and headed over there.

They followed the directions and opened them all at once. Zach and Danielle opened up the ones addressed to Mira and Richard. It mortified them to find a dead crow in each box, not believing what they saw. Jessica's box was the only one that also had a note. It simply stated: *You should have listened to my first warning, now you all will pay.*

Chills went down her spine. She was the only one who knew what the note meant. The letter left on her porch months ago warned her not to return to the island. The same letter had been the only item taken from her house when it was burglarized. After researching symbolism the other day, she knew what the crows meant.

Death. Whoever left the gifts was the same person who left the note, the same person who left the deer carcasses, the same person who left the deer hearts, the same person who tried to kill her and wanted them all dead. Shaking, the tears fell from her eyes. The note falling from her fingertips.

As her body still shook and she struggled to breathe, she told the others about the note through her tears.

"I didn't think. Assuming it was just one of my crazy stalkers from my past. I am so sorry everyone. This is all my fault. I received a note

telling me not to return to the island. Someone had even shut off my generator. Then when my place was burglarized, the only item taken was the note."

Feeling guilty, she had not told them about it before.

"Omg. The night we were on the phone? When your power went out?"

"Yes, I am sorry for not telling you, of all people sooner. I have had stalkers in the past. I just assumed it was one of them again. But, now I know differently."

Timothy wrapped her in a hug and she buried her head in his chest. Everyone assured her it was not her fault, and they sat there trying to brainstorm who it could be.

None of them could think of anyone who would have a motive to hurt the family. There was no gift for Jimmy, however, that wasn't odd. Seeing that it was not public knowledge, he was part of the family. It was only Jimmy that felt the dread of not receiving one. The nagging feeling that he somehow was responsible for the torture occurring to the family just wouldn't go away.

Before heading to bed, they all agreed to bring the gifts to the police the next day. Since they felt it was a direct threat, in context with everything else that had been occurring, they thought it was time to bring in the authorities.

Tossing and turning in his bed, Jimmy struggled to fall asleep. With his mind racing with thoughts of self-doubt. Exhaustion won out, and his eyes shut. His breathing became steady and even. His eyes started rapid movement beneath his eyelids, and he reached a dream state.

He was riding his ATV, and he found the deer carcass again. Staring at the corpse, it morphed into Jessica. He turned and ran, finding himself at the second deer carcass. Which then morphed into Richard Jr. panicking, again he ran stumbling upon the third carcass that morphed into David. Looking at his hands, thick, sticky blood covered them. The smell of rotting flesh was overwhelming. Then, just as he retched, he sat up in bed.

Covered in sweat, Jimmy realized his sheets were soaking wet also. Looking at his hands, he recognized it was just a dreadful nightmare. Getting out of bed, there were no empty beer cans to be seen. That calmed his mind a bit. Still, he needed to make sure everyone in the family was okay. So, he tiptoed to each door and peeked inside to see all were sound asleep.

It was early, but Jimmy knew he couldn't go back to sleep. He stripped his bed of his sheets. Then took a nice hot shower and got dressed for the day. The kitchen was quiet and dark when he entered it. It was too early for Stella to be up preparing breakfast for the family. Making himself a cup of coffee, he looked out the kitchen window. Seeing the light on in Samuel's window above the garage, he wondered what had him up so early.

Then, as he watched, the door to Samuel's

place above the garage opened. Samuel and another person exited. It was dark, so it was hard to tell who the other person was.The couple made their way down the stairs to his truck. Samuel opened the passenger side door and helped the person inside, taking a moment to give them a kiss. Jimmy realized it was a female, and as the door shut to the vehicle, he thought he recognized her. He couldn't be sure, though.

If his eyes weren't deceiving him, he had just seen Rita Duvall get into Samuel's truck. That didn't bode well if their mechanic was having an affair with a very affluent woman from the mainland. Not to mention she was the grandmother of Richard Jr.'s girlfriend.

The thought of Danielle finding out about

her grandmother and Samuel alarmed him. A discussion would have to be had between him and Samuel. Jimmy didn't care so much about the affair. He just cared about the ramifications of it. Already aware of how these matters can lead to messy, unintended consequences.

His thoughts went to how Melissa said the island had a curse. Was she right? Was the land void of morality that led to the destruction of the lives that lived on it? Maybe he should move away, as Melissa did. But the thought of leaving his home and his parents was too much for him to consider. A tear fell down his cheek.

He hadn't felt so lost in a long time. Jimmy would call his therapist later in the day. He hoped he could get help before he descended into the madness of psychosis again. If he hadn't already.

Chapter 19: The fury

They had awakened early to listen to the audio recordings from the party. Smiling as they listened intently to all the secrets the party guests spoke. This one speculating about the eldest Gardiner son and his romantic interest with the mainlander, and that one talking about how peculiar the youngest Gardiner son acted in social scenarios. It was good to know what others thought about the Gardiners. It helped in their plans.

The reappearance of Richard was a hot topic of the party-goers. Some speculated he had actually killed the others on board the sailboat to gain complete control of the island. The only reason people felt he hid away was that Alexandria had not gone on the trip. There was no evidence or bodies to prove or disprove his story that he had told, so people felt they were free to make up their own theories.

Laughing at some conversations overheard about themselves and how they cleaned up well. They had turned a few heads that night and even had a few admirers approaching them. It felt good to be looked at with respect instead of disdain. That feeling fueled the fire and desire for more power.

Just imagining the respect and admiration they would receive when their secret was revealed. It would catapult them into a new hierarchy among the inhabitants and mainlanders alike.

Turning off the recordings from the night before and saving the rest to listen to later, they switched to listening to the family live. The family was still eating breakfast. Their chatter was nauseatingly dull. The family recapped the party from the night before, discussed the food they were eating, and other boorish musings. Nothing was mentioned yet of the mysterious gifts left for the family.

The conversation was too joyous for them to believe the family had already opened the gifts. Instead, they assumed they were waiting to open them until after breakfast. So they sat through the ordinary conversations hoping for just a sliver or slight morsel of a secret.

Disappointed, their heart started racing when they heard the family was done with breakfast and headed into the parlor to unwrap gifts. Waiting as patiently as possible, they suffered through the disgusting exchange of gifts between the family members.

No mention of the gifts they had left. Even when the family finished unwrapping their contributions from one another. Anger built inside them, and they clenched their fists. Why weren't they opening the bequeathed gifts?

They seethed as they listened to the family disperse to do their own things. The family had not followed the instructions to open the gifts altogether. Why? They hadn't even mentioned them.

Determined to discern what went wrong in their plan, they resumed listening to the tapes from the night before. However, it wasn't until they tuned in to Jessica's room recordings they found their answer.

That Bitch! They thought to themselves. She will pay dearly!

Switching back to the live feed to listen in on the family. They suffered through more boorish conversations. Listening to the laughter emanating from the devices made them physically ill. The love shared between the siblings and their significant others made them hate the lot of them even more. It wasn't until much later in the evening they heard Jessica tell Jimmy about the gifts. When the family members took the packages to the security shack, they got up and paced back and forth.

They didn't have listening devices at the security shack. This would mean they wouldn't get the satisfaction of hearing the family's reaction. The fire of rage building inside them was burning to burst out of them.

Grabbing their hunting knife and drone, they left their place for a nighttime hunt. They had perfected attaching the blade to the drone, so it wasn't off balance and could still fly. Using it had made sneaking up on the deer so much easier. Slitting their throats with one swift fly by. Once the deer had fallen and stopped moving, they could cut it open and remove the heart.

Then, using a branch, they covered the tracks they had made with leaves and debris so that it would look as if no one had been there. The light snow that had fallen the night before had all but melted during the day.

Releasing the pent-up anger helped. They felt more powerful again. Their thoughts were calm, and they could think clearly about what needed to be done.

Showering and getting dressed, they decided to have a late-night drink at the mainland bar. They were feeling a bit more adventurous about bringing potential admirers back to their place after the party.

Morning came early, and they knew they needed to get their guest home before it got light out. So, rousing the guest, they drove them home and made it back to the island before too many of the early risers were up and about.

They noticed the Manor house's kitchen light on. Someone was awake early, and they hoped that the house's occupants did not see their comings and goings.

As they ate their breakfast, they smirked, knowing the family may have won the battle on Christmas. However, they would lose the war. In every war, there are casualties. This one would be no different.

They would be victorious in the next battle, and the family would suffer. The casualties would be significant, but first, they needed to lull them into a sense of calm. They learned that the family was already too close-knit and protective of each other. So when they felt threatened, they rallied around one another, and their defenses were more significant than expected.

They had to learn to space out their torture. It would be more fun that way. But just when the family was lulled into a false sense of security, they would need to remind them who was boss.

Chapter 20: Family Matters

The mood at the breakfast table was more subdued than the previous mornings. The siblings had agreed not to discuss the presents in front of their parents. Instead, Jimmy had eaten and rushed out to work. David and Richard Jr. followed closely behind.

They knew their morning would be busy answering questions from the police when they came. Mira and Richard had made plans to spend the day with Lena and Steven. Those plans worked perfectly for the siblings because the police could arrive and do what they needed to do without their parents knowing.

Jessica and Timothy had decided to do

more exploring of the island. They borrowed one radio from the security shack, so they could contact someone if they needed to. Samantha and Danielle were off to work at the café for the day.

Everything seemed normal on the surface of the island until the state police pulled up to the security shack. Jimmy met the officer and walked with him into his office. He closed the door and showed the officer the pictures of the deer carcasses and the hearts. The officer was dismayed and admitted he had seen nothing like that before. When Jimmy showed him the presents left for the family, the officer had no words.

Taking fingerprints would be fruitless, since it had been a day and a half since someone left the presents at the house. Jimmy knew Betty and Martin kept the house spotless and dusted and polished surfaces daily. The police officer and Jimmy went around the island, asking the inhabitants about the deer carcasses to see if they could rattle anyone's cage.

Everyone seemed genuinely upset about the deer carcasses themselves. No one gave any sign they were the ones that killed the deer. Stella broke down in tears when they were questioning her. She never had in her life known of anyone on the island that would have hurt those poor animals.

When they interviewed Betty at the Manor house, she too broke into tears and likened it to finding Ms. Mary in the tub. Jimmy felt terrible since she seemed so shaken up by it all, and it brought up those horrific memories for her.

Samuel even displayed utter disdain for whoever had killed the deer. The police officer took information from Captain Bill about the guests who attended the party and took the ferry across. When he finished, he told Jimmy he wasn't sure what they could do since they had no evidence pointing to who could be tormenting the family.

As the police officer drove away, Jimmy wondered if he should have said something about the beer cans and his own suspicions. Going back to his office and closing the door again, he made the phone call to his therapist. She was more than happy to fit him into her schedule.

Feeling relief that he could talk about what was going through his mind with her, he left the security shack to do his scheduled island rounds. Then, driving towards the windmill to do a security check there, the crackle of his radio startled him.

It was Timothy, and he sounded out of breath and distraught. Once Jimmy could get Timothy to slow down while talking over the radio and not cut himself off. He realized Timothy and Jessica were over by Bostwick Creek, and they needed him to get there ASAP.

When Jimmy pulled up to where Timothy and Jessica were, his heart sank. Their faces told him everything he needed to know without even seeing what they were pointing at. Seeing Jessica's eyes, he read the fear. Timothy had his arm around Jessica protectively.

Zach, Richard Jr., and David on their ATVs in no time joined them. They realized whoever was doing this would not stop. Jimmy briefed them all about what the police officer had said. They all felt defeated. Like they were sitting ducks waiting for the hunter to shoot at them.

They buried the fourth deer carcass, and then they made plans to check Samantha's room every couple of hours. They would have to take turns and not make it clear, so their parents didn't start asking questions.

It was time to head home for dinner by the time they were done. Danielle and Samantha would be home before Mira and Richard, so they knew they could fill them in on the day's events.

Samantha sat on the couch in the parlor with Zach sitting next to her. Danielle sat next to Richard Jr. Jimmy let the two young women know about the police visit and the new deer carcass. Rattled by the news, Samantha cried. Zach put his arm around her, and she leaned her head on his shoulder.

Just when everyone felt a bit defeated, Martin came into the room with a package that had arrived addressed to David. David opened it excitedly, knowing that the contents inside would help them in their quest to determine who was tormenting them.

It was the security cameras. They all felt a bit of relief, and they worked together to figure out where they should go. In no time, they had most of them up and running. They had several on the outside of the house and a few on the inside. Making sure the cameras were not noticeable, they felt more confident and safer.

When their parents came home, the group was more relaxed playing pool and having fun. Mira and Richard were unaware of the family's dangers and enjoyed watching the young adults having fun.

Jimmy refrained from even having a beer at the advice of his therapist. The phone session had been helpful, and Jimmy felt a little more at ease. She had commended him for recognizing potential signs of an impending break. Assuring him, she didn't think he was having one, but it was good that he reached out for help, just in case.

When the others questioned why he

wasn't having a beer, he just shrugged it off as wanting to start the new year on a healthier note. They had all agreed that they could all do with being a bit more healthy and also refrained from drinking that evening.

The following morning Jimmy was happy to awake to no empty beer cans. As the morning progressed and finding no deer's heart anywhere near Samantha's room, everyone seemed to relax a bit more. Finally, Samantha and Danielle headed off to work, as Jimmy, David, and Richard Jr. also did.

They left Timothy and Jessica with her parents, who had taken it upon themselves to set up some appointments to meet with caterers and bakers for the wedding. So naturally, Jessica was a little more than annoyed. Yet, she bit her tongue and went along with the plans.

Her parents started talking about serving caviar and pate at the first caterers. This was when Jessica had had enough. It was her wedding, after all.

"We do not want caviar or pate. Timothy and I like neither of those things, and we do not want something that we dislike at our wedding. Sorry to disappoint, but we want simple finger foods. We want a choice of three entrees. A fish dish, a chicken dish, and a beef dish. Nothing too fancy."

Timothy shifted a bit in his seat. This was the first time he had seen Jessica lose her temper. There was no blame on her, and Timothy was glad she spoke up. Bracing for the potential backlash from her parents, he reached for her hand to let her know he supported her.

Both Mira and Richard sat with mouths agape and eyes wide. Mira was a bit more wounded-looking, and her bottom lip trembled ever so slightly. Richard furrowed his brows and rubbed his hand along his chin.

The caterer sat across from them, frozen mid-turning of a page. Not knowing whether to proceed or step out of the room and let the clients have a moment of privacy.

"I apologize, Jessica. Your mother and I seem to have overstepped our boundaries. Of course, we do not mean to. But Timothy, we owe you both an apology. We are truly sorry."

"Look, Mom and Dad, I appreciate your enthusiasm in helping us plan our wedding and all. But we grew up differently than you did. Our tastes and styles are different. We accept your

apology."

"Dear, we had to have a small wedding because of many circumstances. So we have gotten caught up in the idea of throwing you a big glamourous wedding that we never had. We are sorry."

"Mom, I know you mean well. I do. We are just very different from you. I would be perfectly content with a small backyard wedding."

Timothy relaxed. He felt that clearing the air had helped ease the tension felt in the past with Jessica's parents. Jessica also relaxed. She felt better about finally getting her feelings out in the open with her parents. It surprised her they took it so well.

Mira and Richard sat quietly as Jessica and Timothy discussed options with the caterer. When they finished, they had received a detailed quote. The following two caterers went smoothly, with Mira and Richard letting Jessica and Timothy do all the talking.

By the end of the day, they decided which caterer they would go with and the menu that would be served. Jessica and Timothy felt good about getting that settled and out of the way.

When everyone was back at the Manor house for the evening, Jessica set up her photography equipment to take the family photos she had promised to take. First, she took a few of just her and her siblings. Some of her parents, her siblings, and herself. Then she took a couple with Timothy, Jimmy, Zach, and Danielle all in there, too.

It was another fun-filled, relaxing evening, and they all went to bed feeling as if the craziness of the last few days was all over.

Timothy and Jessica were lying in bed. He raised himself up on his elbow and looked at Jessica proudly.

"Babe, I can't believe you finally stood up to your parents. I know it was hard, but I think it was the best thing for all of us."

"Thanks, I just couldn't hold it all in anymore. Especially with all the other stress we are going through. I know they don't know about all that, but I just needed to clear the air."

"I've got to admit, though, you were pretty scary. That was my first time seeing you so angry. I never want to see you like that again. Remind me not to piss you off!"

Jessica laughed and pushed him onto his

back.

"That's right, Mr. Sullivan, don't get on my bad side. It won't bode well for you!"

Reaching up to pull her to him, Timothy kissed her lips softly.

"I never want to get on your bad side, not because I fear you, but because your good side is just so good!"

Jessica stroked his hair lovingly while looking him squared in the eyes and smirked. Then she kissed him tenderly. It wasn't long before they were fast asleep in each other's arms.

Chapter 21: The Late Gift

After the New Year, everyone had to get back to their respective routines. So Jessica and Timothy said goodbye to her family and headed back to Connecticut. As Jessica sat in the passenger seat, she watched the scenery go past her window. Although things had started off crazy during this visit to the island, things had calmed down, and it had actually turned out pretty good. After the blowout with her parents and the ensuing discussion, she felt better about her relationship. In addition, sharing the experiences with her siblings and cousin solidified her gratefulness for finding her biological family.

Timothy had gotten a call from his editor the day before, asking them to go to Ireland to do a piece on plants that survive the winter there. It would be a quick trip home to unpack from the holiday and pack for their Ireland trip. Jessica had been to Ireland only a few months before and was looking forward to returning. It was one of her favorite countries to visit. However, this time would be unique because Timothy would be with her.

Richard and Mira headed back to their home in Boston. The mood in their car was melancholy. They were both coming to terms with their adult children's choices. Mira quietly contemplated what it would mean to not have her kids at home or even close by. It would be a new chapter in their lives and in their relationship.

She and Richard had been together for so long. They had children quickly in their relationship. So they really hadn't had time as just a couple. Sure, they had the moments they stole behind everyone's backs in the beginning.

That was exciting to both of them. Holding each other as a secret. But keeping the secret of Richard's true identity for so long had given their relationship a constant sense of excitement. Wondering if their secrets would ever be discovered.

Now the entire world knew, and they were just an ordinary couple. Mira didn't know how she felt about that. Looking over at Richard, she still felt those butterflies in her stomach. He had aged well. Grey hairs peppered throughout his dirty blonde hair. His piercing blue eyes still made her weak in the knees, just as they did when she was a schoolgirl. The thought of having more time alone with her husband made her appreciate the new opportunities presented to them by their children's decisions.

Looking in the car's side-view mirror, she saw Samantha and Zach following behind them to pack up Samantha's things to move her into the Manor house.

Driving Samantha's car, Zach followed behind her parents. Samantha looked out the window and then over at Zach. She was so enamored with him. Never in a million years did Samantha ever think finding her soulmate would happen while waitressing.

Sure she had dated other guys before him.

None that Samantha had met while working, though. Most had been in high school, and the rest she usually met through friends of friends.

The quiet kindness and respect Zach always gave her was a stark contrast to previous guys from her dating history. However, their relationship had blossomed quickly, and with it, she had a newfound understanding of her sister's relationship with Timothy. Discussing their relationships with each other had strengthened the bond between sisters. Samantha felt blessed that they had found her big sister.

Samantha realized fate had played a significant role in both of their relationships. However, this differed from their brother's current situation. His connection with Danielle had begun as children and grew organically over the years. While the family situation had moved the process along, there was no doubt in Samantha's mind that Richard Jr. and Danielle would have ended up together, anyway. Their kinship was destiny.

David had the day off and had made plans to hang out with Joe, the bartender from the party. It was the first time they could hang out since they had first met. Discovering that they both enjoyed bowling, they went, so they had a chance to talk more.

The closest bowling alley was in Riverhead. Driving together gave the men more opportunity to get to know one another. David was enjoying Joe's companionship. It was easy between them. He had opened up to Joe about his conflicting feelings about his sexuality at the party.

Joe was completely understanding. This made David feel less alone and accepted than he had ever felt. It was a good feeling. For the first time in a long time, David thought it was okay not to be sure of himself. He took Stella's advice, just being who he was and letting life flow freely.

Jimmy had to work. Richard Jr. and Danielle stayed back at the Manor house. They both had the day off. Danielle was secretly hoping that since things had quieted down, she and Richard Jr. could take their relationship to the next level.

Danielle had planned out their afternoon. First, she had asked Stella to make a picnic-style lunch in a basket and all. Then, when it was ready, she sent Richard Jr. down to get it. Hoping Stella would remember her instructions to stall him from immediately coming back upstairs.

The candles she wanted to place around the room hid in a bag under the bed. As she got them out, her heart pounded in her chest. This needed to be perfect. Strategically, she placed a few candles in the fireplace across from the four-poster bed. Then she put a few on the mantel and on the bureau in the room. Each side table had one candle placed on it as well.

Quickly she went around, lighting the candles. The scent of vanilla promptly permeated the room. She knew she had little time left, so she spread the checkerboard patterned blanket in front of the fireplace and then went into the bathroom to change.

Richard Jr. returned to the room with the basket. Smiling when he saw the candles and the blanket. Taking the cue from how Danielle had set up the room and spreading the basket lunch on the throw. He then poured them each a glass of the Merlot from the bottle placed in the basket by Stella at Danielle's request.

As Danielle opened the door to the bathroom, Richard Jr.'s breath was taken away at the sight of her. She was wearing a long, flowing red satin dress with spaghetti straps. The satin clung to her body and showed every curve.

"I saved your best Christmas present for last. I hope you don't mind it being late." Danielle

walked over and took a seat next to Richard Jr. on the blanket.

Richard Jr.'s heart raced in his chest. He was feeling so conflicted. His desire for Danielle was strong, and he wanted to act on all those impulses. Yet, his brain flooded his mind with the *what ifs* of taking their relationship to the next level. Losing Danielle would rock his world. He realized she was ready for the next level in their relationship, but was he?

He didn't want to disappoint Danielle. She had clearly gone to a lot of trouble to put this all together for them. Would he disappoint her if his heart wasn't fully ready for this step? If he turned down her advances, could it hurt their relationship? Would she feel as though he didn't love her enough?

The pause in Richard Jr.'s response concerned Danielle. Was he ready for this step? He was such an overthinker. The one quality that she had issues with about him. Sometimes she wished he would just be more spontaneous and not so concerned with what might happen. She wanted him to learn to live in the moment.

"I love you and the present. No, I don't mind it being late."

Richard Jr. handed her a glass of wine.

He followed the wine by offering her a chocolate-covered strawberry. She bit into it while he was still holding it. Then, they took turns feeding each other their lunch. Before they knew it, Richard Jr. tipped the wine bottle to pour more wine into Danielle's glass. The last drop of the wine slowly rolled into Danielle's glass. Finally, they had finished the bottle of Merlot and the last bites of their lunch.

Richard Jr. Stood up and reached his hand out to Danielle. Pulling her up into his arms, he let go of any thoughts he was having and gave in to his desires. Scooping her up in his arms, he carried her over to the bed and gave her what she craved most of him.

When they were done, they lay quietly in each other's arms. There were no more doubts in Richard Jr.'s mind. This was what he wanted for the rest of his life. He just prayed it was what Danielle wanted as well. Then, the constant overthinker made plans for their future.

Later in the evening, they joined Jimmy for dinner. Jimmy had ridden the ATV all day, making security rounds, and caught up with Richard Jr. on the day's developments. It wasn't much. Things had seemed to quiet down a bit, and the fourth deer's heart had not shown up anywhere. That had been a considerable relief to them all.

They attributed the quiet to the installation of the cameras. While they felt they had placed them in hidden areas, it was the only reason the torture had stopped. But, except in Jimmy's mind, there was another explanation.

He had stopped drinking altogether and had talked to his therapist again regularly. But, unfortunately, this information was not shared with his cousins. So they all thought that somehow the person responsible for terrorizing the family had found out about the cameras.

They were all happy the terror had stopped. Being more relaxed was helping them all settle into a routine on the island. After dinner, Jimmy challenged Richard Jr. to a game of pool. Danielle contemplating, watched.

Richard Jr. seemed different, in a good way. He kissed her a few times between turns and called her his good luck charm. The spontaneity of affection publicly was something he had never done in the past. She smiled at her wish coming true. Winning the first game, Richard Jr. then challenged Martin, who had joined them in the parlor.

After winning a few more rounds of pool, Richard Jr. announced he was retiring for the evening. Then, taking Danielle's hand, he led her upstairs to his bedroom. While lying beside her in bed, he propped himself up on one arm, facing her.

"I think you should officially move in with me."

"Don't you have to check with Jessica and Jimmy?"

"Of course, but I need to know if you will or not before I even bother with that step."

And there was the overthinking again. Danielle smiled, knowing he wouldn't change completely, especially in one day.

"Well, I practically live here anyway, so why not? It isn't like I will take up a whole other bedroom. And it will be good for Samantha to have another woman in this house of men."

"*Then it's settled. I will talk to Jimmy and Jessica tomorrow, although I do not see them objecting to it.*"

Leaning over, he gently kissed her lips. Danielle returned the kiss with passion and fire running through her veins. They made love until they were both exhausted and craved sleep.

Chapter 22: Ireland Escape

It was 5:00 am when Jessica and Timothy landed in Dublin, Ireland. They claimed their baggage and then headed to the rental car desk. Jessica was excited to show Timothy around this beautiful city. They had never assigned him to write anything in Ireland before, so it was his first time on the Emerald Isle. Jessica had been there multiple times, including a few short months ago.

Excitement filled Jessica, and Timothy loved watching how she hurried to get through all the rental car paperwork. Since Timothy had never driven on the opposite side of the road before, they agreed Jessica should be the one to drive.

Driving to the Crowne Plaza, the hotel they were staying overnight in, they hoped they could check in early. The desk clerk was more than gracious, letting them check in to their room. They both felt the need to take a quick nap, and then they would explore Dublin for the rest of the day.

When they got up, they both showered and got ready to start the day of exploring. First, they walked to the corner and caught a bus into the heart of the city. From there, they bought tickets for the Do Dublin Hop-on Hop-off bus tour.

Timothy, who was used to New York City, was amazed at the cleanliness of the buildings and streets in Dublin. However, he understood

Jessica's love of the old and new blend of architecture. It definitely gave the vibe of stepping back in time with the modern conveniences.

They hopped on the bus at O'Connell street and hopped off for the first stop at Parnell Square North. Jessica figured Timothy would enjoy going to the Dublin Writers Museum. Timothy could appreciate the Irish literary tradition displayed proudly throughout the museum as a writer. Hopping back on the bus where they got off, they looked at the map and planned their next hop.

Choosing to check out the Natural History Museum next, they hopped off at Merrion Street Upper. The walking they needed to do to get to their destinations daunted neither of them. The people they met along the way were friendly, and the crowds were nowhere near what they encountered back home in New York City.

After touring the museum, they found a quaint Irish bar called Foleys. Jessica loved the blue façade surrounding the doors, and as she stepped into the place, she felt transported in time. The colorful bar stools and high-top tables added an air of Irish whimsy. While the fireplace added warmth and ambiance.

They were seated by their server and were given menus to look over. Everything looked delicious. Settling on the fish and chips, they both ordered a beer and waited for their food to arrive.

The difference in Jessica here was so noticeable to Timothy. Although he had a hard time pinpointing exactly what it was. Her eyes seemed to sparkle with a bit of magic that he hadn't seen back in the states. There was a glow around her that radiated from within.

"Let's stay here for a bit after we are done with our assignment."

Not even knowing where the idea had come from. Timothy just knew he didn't want to rush away from this place.

"You were reading my mind. I will do you one better. Let's look for a home here in the country. A retreat we can come to whenever we want."

By the end of their lunch, they had booked the rest of the month at various stops in Ireland. They would meet with their tour guide the next day to show them the plants they were there to do the article on. They didn't expect the assignment to take long at all to complete. Timothy had already done research on the subject. It was only a matter of interviewing people with knowledge of the plants, their uses, and the pictures.

Rounding out their afternoon, they visited St. Patrick's Cathedral, the Teeling Whiskey Distillery, and Guinness Storehouse. The drivers of the Do Dublin bus tour made the trip entertaining, telling stories about the city and the history behind it all, embellishing along the way. When Jessica and Timothy returned to their hotel, they were exhausted.

For the next couple of days, Jessica and Timothy spent completing their assignment. When they were done, they turned their attention to looking for the perfect place to purchase as their getaway retreat. They drove throughout the country until they came across the small townland of Manorhamilton in the county of Leitrim.

Something about the quaint main street lined with small shops and pubs felt like home for both of them. They stayed in a small bed-and-breakfast, and they met with a realtor to show them properties in the area. It wasn't long before they found the perfect cottage with several acres and a few outbuildings.

The road leading to the cottage was dirt and narrow. Stone walls lined both sides of the alley. There were rolling hills peppered with sheep grazing.

"It reminds me a little of home, doesn't it?"

"Yes, it does Jessica. I understand why you

love it here so much."

Jessica wanted to share the news with her siblings, especially Samantha. Yet, on the other hand, she desired to keep it a secret. She knew Samantha would adore the cottage and would help her decorate it perfectly.

Samantha had a flair for knowing just what Jessica liked or disliked. It was amazing how the two sisters seemed to just meld into one person when they were with each other. The more they got to know each other. The more they freaked everyone around them out with their uncanny ability to finish each other's sentences and read each other's minds.

By the time Timothy and Jessica got back to Connecticut, it was the beginning of February. Jessica missed her sister immensely and made plans to do a girls' weekend after Valentine's Day.

Jessica had told Samantha about the Ireland retreat and swore her to secrecy for the time being. Jessica felt the need to keep this bit of news from the rest of the family. She didn't understand her gut feeling that she would need this retreat in the future, but the inkling was there. Until she could discern why, she had the feeling, though, she would keep it under wraps.

Samantha loved having secrets with her sister, so she gladly agreed to keep it. She didn't need a reason. If her big sister asked her to keep a secret, she would no matter what.

The only other female Samantha was close to was Danielle, Richard Jr.'s live-in girlfriend. Jimmy and Jessica had agreed it would be okay for her to move in. Samantha really appreciated having another female in the Manor house.

Samantha and Zach hadn't made the commitment to live with each other yet. Samantha was still adjusting to moving out of her parent's home into the Manor house with her brothers and cousin Jimmy.

She felt that there was a closer bond with her brothers now than when they were younger. Yet, her bond with her sister was the strongest. She and Jessica had discussed this frequently since they met. Neither could explain the instantaneous connection they had. They both felt it deep in their souls, though, and they knew it was an unbreakable bond.

Because of this bond, Jessica knew her secret Ireland retreat was safe with Samantha. Timothy agreed it was best to keep the new purchase under wraps for now. He also had an unwavering feeling that someday it might be necessary to hide away there. Even though it had been quiet since Christmas day, Timothy still felt Jessica was in danger. He would do everything possible to keep her safe.

Chapter 23: Happy And Sad News

Samantha was getting ready for her date with Zach. It was Valentine's Day, and they were going to the mainland for dinner. They had been dating for almost two months now. Choosing her outfit was becoming difficult, and she wished her sister was there to help.

Finally settling on a pair of jeans and a blue v-neck sweater with a white tank top underneath. Again, she felt comfortable, but pretty. Finally, she decided on a pair of brown short-cut boots.

Zach was always punctual, and this time was no different. Martin called up to Samantha to let her know her suitor had arrived. As she walked down the staircase, Zach let out a whistle. She blushed and laughed, remembering how he did most of the blushing in the early stages of their relationship.

Kissing him on the cheek when she reached him at the bottom of the stairs, it was Zach's turn to do the blushing. Zach handed her a bouquet of carnations. They were red, pink, and white with a few sprigs of baby's breath. She thanked him and gave the flowers to Martin to put in a vase.

After helping Samantha with her coat, Zach made sure she was nice and warm before they headed out into the blustery cold. They made it to the mainland and headed to the 1777 Restaurant Tavern.

The hostess seated them at a corner table

when they entered the restaurant. It was pretty busy, and Zach was glad he had made reservations. In January, they had both turned 21, so they started off with some Pino Grigio and some appetizers.

When their entrees came, they were both feeling the effects of the wine. They both ordered another glass. They giggled amongst themselves as they ate, drank, and people watched.

People watching made them realize they knew a lot of the customers in the place. They saw Betty and presumably her date for the evening. Jimmy was there entertaining a young woman. Even Samuel was there, but they could not see who he was with. Much to both of their surprise, Samantha's brothers were there with Danielle and Joe for the evening.

Richard Jr. and Danielle were sitting across the room at another table in a corner. Richard Jr. seemed nervous. However, Danielle didn't notice and was discussing something with him.

As they watched, Richard seemed to drop his fork on the floor, and he got up from his chair to get it. When he moved the chair and got down on one knee, though, Samantha realized what he was about to do.

Patting Zach's arm frantically, Samantha pointed over at Richard Jr. and Danielle's table. Sitting there eagerly watching the scene unfold in front of them, they intertwined their hands together, praying Danielle would say yes.

Watching Danielle's face as it registered what was happening was priceless. She covered her mouth with her hands.

Richard Jr. looked into Danielle's eyes.

"Danielle, you have been my best friend since we were children. I can't imagine my life without you. Will you marry me?"

When Danielle uncovered her mouth and said yes, the entire tavern erupted in cheers and applause. It had gone quiet when everyone had noticed what Richard Jr. was about to do.

Samantha and Zach hurriedly went over and congratulated the newly engaged couple. David and Joe also joined in on the congratulations. Betty and her date were just leaving and stopped by the table to congratulate them. They were all surprised when Samuel and

Rita approached the table to congratulate the couple also.

Rita, Danielle's grandmother, had recently filed for divorce. The fact she was out with Samuel didn't seem appropriate to Danielle. Not wanting to ruin the moment, she kept her opinion to herself. Sensing discomfort, Rita and Samuel didn't linger long at the table of the engaged couple.

Zach and Samantha returned to their table and finished their dinner and their glasses of wine. They ordered a dessert and a cup of coffee to sober up a bit. Both were feeling quite tipsy, and they knew neither of them were okay to drive.

Even after dessert and coffee, they both felt very disoriented. The only person still there that they knew was Jimmy. Sitting at the bar with his date, they didn't want to interfere.

Samantha and Zach both had difficulty walking to Zach's car. First, they debated whether they should try to get a room there at the Inn for the night. Then they figured it was probably already booked full because of Valentine's Day.

Sitting in the car, both felt their eyes were getting heavy. Samantha couldn't form words anymore, and Zach couldn't hear anything but muffled voices. Not recognizing where or who the voices were coming from. He couldn't even tell if one voice was his.

Danielle and Richard Jr. had gone to her parent's house to show them the ring. They had known he would propose because Richard had asked for permission earlier in the week. Lena and Steven were ecstatic, and Danielle's sisters were fawning over her and the ring.

It was a magical night for the happy couple. They couldn't wait to plan the wedding.

David and Joe had left the tavern and went to Joe's apartment after congratulating the newly engaged couple. They had been hanging out for a month now and tonight was their first official date. To anyone watching them, they looked like two friends hanging out. However, only the two of them were aware they were calling this a date.

David was still unsure of his sexuality, but Joe made him feel comfortable about his uncertainty. They could talk about anything. This was why David had finally agreed to go on an actual date with him. Joe was very sure of his sexuality and had made it very clear to David there was an attraction.

As they settled on the couch to watch a movie, Joe put his arm around David. He knew David wasn't sure of the physical aspects of their relationship, so he wanted to take things slowly and one step at a time. David didn't flinch or pull away. Instead, he felt content and safe. So he leaned in and put his head on Joe's shoulder.

It was late, and David was too tired to drive home when the movie was over. Joe got him a pillow and blanket and set him up on the couch. As much as Joe wanted to share his bed with David, he wasn't sure David was prepared for that yet.

Joe cared enough about David to wait until he was ready and confident about what he wanted. Finding yourself was never easy. Realizing you were a homosexual was even harder, only because of society and the negative connotations.

Joe knew it all too well. Caring about David, he wanted to help him through this challenging period in his life. Indeed, he didn't want to add to David's confusion about his autonomy and identity.

Jimmy left the tavern with his date for the evening. As he opened the car door for her and helped her into the passenger side of his car, he recognized Zach's car still in the corner of the parking lot. The windows were pretty fogged up, so he assumed Zach and Samantha were just being bold and having a marathon make-out session in the parking lot.

It wasn't until the following morning when the state police came knocking on the door to the Manor house. He found out he was dead wrong. Martin had let the police sergeant in and then went to get Jimmy.

Jimmy at first thought the police officer was there with a lead who had been terrorizing and threatening the family months ago.

"Mr. Driscoll, does a Samantha Gardiner live here? And does Zach Zimmerman live on the island?"

Remembering the night before and thinking they must have gotten themselves into trouble with indecent exposure or something.

Jimmy chuckled.

"Yes, Samantha lives here, and Zach lives down the road. So what trouble did they get themselves into?"

"Well, sir, the kind they can't get themselves out of. We found them in the young man's car this morning. Seems they got themselves mixed up with some dangerous drugs. Overdosed. We found them with needles still sticking in their arms."

Jimmy's head spun. He sat himself down on the stairs in the entranceway.

"Overdosed? Needles? Drugs? They both just turned 21 a few weeks ago. They were just drinking. There must be some mistake."

Jimmy choked out as he cried.

"I am sorry, sir. Preliminary findings are no

other fingerprints other than the victims on the needles. Of course, the coroner will do an autopsy. Can you point me toward the young man's home so I can notify his family?"

Jimmy gave the officer the address of Zach's parents. He followed him over to the house. Standing beside the officer as he delivered the devastating news, he could barely watch as he saw Zach's mom fall to her knees on the floor. The wailing that came from the depths of her soul was unbearable to watch. Matt gently kneeled next to his wife and held her as he also sobbed.

Jimmy somberly returned to the Manor house to face the daunting task of telling Samantha's brothers she was dead.

Chapter 24: Notifications

David was driving up to the Manor house. The state trooper was leaving, and he could see Jimmy getting off his ATV. The sweat on his palms made it hard to grip the steering wheel. David could tell the trooper's visit wasn't a good one, watching Jimmy's movements. Jimmy looked frazzled, and as he got closer, it looked as if he was crying. They had all been through some pretty harrowing times together. But never had he seen Jimmy in such a state.

The anticipation made David's heart race. What could have his cousin so distraught? Jimmy stopped short of the back kitchen door, noticing David's car pulling up. His shoulders raised and dropped as he breathed a tremendous sigh, preparing himself for what he had to do.

Meeting David at his car, he waited for him to park and get out.

"Man, what's got you in such a tizzy, bro? Another carcass."

"I... wish... Samantha... and Zach... they both. They're gone, kid. An overdose or something."

Jimmy stammered out the words. Then he grabbed his younger cousin in a big bear hug as he finished.

David could not process what was just said. An aching in his chest worsened with each second that passed. His mind was numb. The only thing that told him this wasn't a dream was his cousin's arms around him. His eyes welled up. He melted into his cousin as his breathing hurt, and he sobbed.

The two cousins stood there for what seemed like an eternity. They helped each other into the house. Faced with Danielle and Richard Jr. staring at them as they walked into the kitchen.

Danielle's face went from glowing and smiling to concern for why the two men seemed unhinged. Richard Jr. also went from a jovial expression to one of worry.

David walked up to his big brother and hugged him harder than he ever had. As he did, he broke into another round of sobs. Richard

Jr. hugged his little brother back, not knowing why David wouldn't let go.

He had never seen his little brother this way. Not knowing how to react, Richard Jr. squeezed as hard as possible. David reciprocated, pressing him back. The unusual exchange between brothers only added to the eldest brother's confusion.

"Richard, I... don't... know... how ..."

Jimmy was trying to get the words out between his own tears.

"Jimmy, just tell me what the hell is going on?"

"Samantha and Zach..."

David pulled away from his brother as he gave him the news.

"They are dead! They're gone."

Richard Jr. felt as if he was going to get sick. His baby sister, dead. Too many questions ran through his head. Then he felt Danielle's arms around him and her body shaking with tears of grief.

"They were just fine last night!! What happened? How? Please don't tell me the psychopath got them."

"The police have ruled it an accidental overdose. They found them in Zach's car this morning. No signs of foul play. I know. It makes little sense."

Nothing about this felt right. Richard Jr. felt as if he was in a horrible nightmare. Balling up his fists, he pounded them on the counter. And then came the tears. He couldn't be strong a minute more. Breaking into full sobs, he crumpled to the floor. Danielle sat next to him and just held him, crying with him.

The news spread over the island. The shock seen and felt in the inhabitant's faces. Everyone rallied around Zach's parents while Jimmy set out to tell Jessica and Timothy in person. He just couldn't tell them over the phone. Richard Jr., David, and Danielle headed to Boston to inform their parents.

The long trip to Connecticut was torturous for Jimmy. He didn't know how he was going to tell Jessica. Imagining how devastated she was going to be made his stomach turn.

Only knowing his cousins for a short time, they still had bonded in a flash. Jessica and Samantha had been like two peas in a pod. Instant best friends. He knew this would shake

Jessica to her core. It had shaken him to his crux. Samantha was his cousin, and Zach was not just an employee. He had been a friend and like a brother to him. Losing both of them ripped at his soul.

Jimmy wanted to numb the hurt. He hadn't craved alcohol or even drugs for years. Although, right now, Jimmy felt the descent into the depths of hell could occur at any moment. He texted his therapist as he sat on the ferry crossing the Long Island Sound.

The therapist responded in short order, and the entire ferry ride across the sound, they had a texting session. In the end, Jimmy felt better and not as out of control as before reaching out to her. He was still dreading notifying Jessica of Samantha's death.

The ride to Jessica and Timothy's seemed to take forever, and as he drove up the driveway, his stomach lurched. He needed to keep it together.

Jessica heard the tires coming up the driveway. The hair on the back of her neck stood up. Every fiber of her being sensed impending danger or doom. It was out of the ordinary for them to have unannounced visitors. But, looking at Timothy, she could also see a bit of alarm and concern in him. They both peeked out the window and recognized Jimmy's truck coming to a stop.

This was not a planned visit, so Jessica knew off the bat something was wrong. She and Timothy met Jimmy at the door. He didn't even ring the doorbell or even knock.

Jessica sized him up. He looked like he had aged five years in the month she hadn't seen him. His eyes were puffy and bloodshot. The disheveled look of his hair, as if he had been running his hands through it. Jessica knew this was a habit of his, in stressful situations.

"Hey, Jimmy, what brings you all the way out here?"

She saw him tremble as he stepped inside the house. His hands went through his hair as he walked to the living room and sat down. His thoughts raced, and he couldn't find the words to tell her. He couldn't shatter her heart.

"Jimmy?"

As she watched her cousin's bizarre behavior. Dread overcome her, sitting next to him on the couch. She put her hand on his knee.

Jessica's touch startled him. He looked at her and saw the genuine concern in her green eyes. Yet, the fear was there too, and he knew that deep down, she knew something terrible had happened.

Jimmy drew in a deep breath and looked his cousin in the eyes as he told her what had happened to Samantha and Zach.

Jessica couldn't breathe. She hadn't heard him correctly, had she? Jessica knew what he was saying was true, though feeling it in her soul. Getting up, she ran out the back door and dropped into the snow on her knees. Looking up at the sky, she screamed as her body shook with grief, and she sobbed.

Timothy ran out after her and encircled

her in his arms. Soon he realized the coldness of the snow, and he helped Jessica back into the house.

Jimmy didn't stay long. He headed back home to the island, and for the first time in his life, he contemplated not going back. Again, he understood what Melissa had said about the island, feeling as if there was a curse. Melissa, she would come to the funeral. So he assumed, at least. But, oh, God, how could he face her after the drunken proposal? Would she even step foot on the island, thinking that would send a message of acceptance to him if she did? He had made a mess of things.

As Jimmy traveled back to the island, Richard, Jr., Danielle, and David were just pulling into their parent's home driveway. None of them wanted to get out of the car. They seemed frozen in place. Richard Jr. sighed and opened the car door. The others followed his lead.

It was the first time he had been back at his childhood home since he had moved out. These were not the circumstances he had wanted to return for. But, as he went to knock on the door, it opened in a swift motion.

Mira and Richard had heard the car pull into the driveway. They were excited to congratulate Richard Jr. and Danielle on their engagement. Assuming that was what the surprise visit was for, since Richard Jr. had called them to tell them the news the night before.

Richard Jr. stood confused as his mother and father enveloped him in a friendly hug and stated their congratulations to both Richard Jr.

and Danielle. It wasn't until his parents regis-tered David was also with them. Along with Danielle and Richard Jr.'s stiff response to the congratulations, Mira sensed another reason for their visit.

"What is wrong?"

Richard Jr., David, and Danielle ushered Mira and Richard back into the house, closing the door behind them. Making sure their par-ents were sitting before telling them the dread-ful news.

It seemed like an eternity that it took for what they said to register with Mira and Rich-ard. The color drained from their mother's face as it sunk in. Richard wrapped his arm around Mira and pulled her to him. As he did, Mira broke and, through her sobs, kept repeating.

"NO, NO, NO!"

Danielle, Richard Jr., and David stayed the night at the house since they all couldn't function. They would head back to the island in the morning to help with the funeral arrangements.

Mira seemed to go into a bit of a trance and went through the motions of getting the guest beds ready for her children. Afterward, she retired to her own bedroom, where the others could hear her sobs through the door.

She refused to come down for breakfast and see her children off in the morning. Richard, however, hugged his sons and his daughter-in-law to be extra tight as he said goodbye. Then, as he watched them drive away, he contemplated if he had done the right thing coming out of hiding and taking control of his share of the inheritance.

Sitting in his living room, he put his head in his hands and cried. The guilt washed over him. Was this karma for the deaths of his cousins so long ago? His beautiful Samantha, named after his beloved cousin Samuel, taken from him at such a young age. He did not lose the irony.

The thought of giving up his entire inheritance crossed his mind. It wouldn't bring his little girl back from the grave. However, maybe it would stop the karma that seemed to have been set in motion.

Chapter 25: Re-evaluating plans

They had heard the news through the grapevine on the island. But, of course, they pretended to be shocked and sad when they were told. Some part of high school had paid off, at least. They had become very good at acting through their years of theatre classes.

The deaths of Samantha and Zach were not a shock to them. They relished the fact that they had been successful again in killing their victims and making it look like something other than murder. The power surged through their veins.

It had all worked out so perfectly. They had heard the family's plans. Knowing they would all be at the same restaurant, even when they all didn't know each other would be there.

The engagement plans fit perfectly since they knew it would provide the perfect distraction to add something to Samantha and Zach's drinks to enhance the effects of the alcohol they were drinking. The only gamble had been making sure their own date was home safe before they returned with the syringes.

The gamble had paid off. The couple was still there, sitting in the parking lot, when they returned. They laughed, remembering how completely out of it both of their victims had been. When they had offered the syringes as a cure to their hangovers, they both jumped at the chance. Little had the two naïve victims known the syringes contained fatal doses of heroin and fentanyl.

The pair had so willingly shot themselves in the arm. It was almost comical. As they had watched, the pair's lips turned blue within seconds. Their breathing gurgled, and as their bodies stiffened, they foamed at the mouth and went unresponsive.

They had felt for a pulse on both of them to ensure they indeed had expired. Neither Samantha nor Zach had any sign of life as they left them in the car to be found by whoever might stumble upon them.

The joy they felt in realizing that they were one step closer to their goal was over-whelming. It almost made them giddy. Soon enough, the entire family would be gone, and they could take their rightful place on the island.

They would have it all, the island, the Manor house, the inheritance. Everything would be theirs. The power would be theirs. The control would be theirs.

No one could stop them. No one even suspected them. The police had ruled Samantha and Zach's deaths an accidental overdose. They had been meticulous not to be seen doing anything.

Just knowing they had gotten away with murder again emboldened them. They needed to kill again, sooner rather than later. They craved the surge of energy that came with each kill. It couldn't be an animal either.

That had become mundane and boring. The next kill needed another human, and it needed to be another one of the family members. The question was, which one would they take next?

Would it be the youngest boy David? They had found he had secrets of his own. Those secrets could definitely come in handy in their master plan.

The oldest boy had just gotten engaged, which posed another threat to their plans. That added another heir to the mix when they got married. Two couples engaged. That made the elimination of them a chief priority.

Then the matter of the parents being so far away. They had hoped that with the children all moving to the island, mommy and daddy would follow suit. They had heard the conversation between Mira and Richard. Mira had no desire to move to the island. Maybe it was time to arrange a need to live on the island. That would make it so much easier for them to accomplish their plans.

Not to mention the possibility of any unplanned pregnancies occurring. The immorality of the family was the reason for so many buried secrets. It would be the downfall of them all. The Gardiner children were all just as immoral. Could they kill a child if it came down to it? They needed to make contingency plans just in case.

If another life posed a threat to their ultimate plans, that life needed to be eliminated. No matter what.

They felt they were the one chosen to restore balance and morality to the island.

They were feeling more powerful every day.

Chapter 26: Preparing to Say Goodbye

Jessica and Timothy prepared to head back to the island to say goodbye to Samantha and Zach. Jessica had not stopped crying for days. Every time she thought she was done, something would remind her of the gut-wrenching sorrow she felt.

When she heard her sister's favorite song on the radio, she tried to sing along like Samantha always had, but she ended up choking back the tears. Then, walking past the fireplace mantel and seeing the picture of her and Samantha taken at Christmas would stop her in her tracks, and the tears would start again.

Repeatedly, she would apologize to Timothy for her constant tears. He would tell her it was okay, and he was there for her forever. Feeling blessed, she had him in her life. However, also feeling guilty, he had to endure her depressive state. Every night she fell asleep in his arms, crying.

The sadness she felt was so deep. She had never felt such a profound loss. Yes, she had mourned the loss of her adoptive parents, and she had been sad. But this, this grief cut deep in her heart. She didn't know if she would ever recover from it. The soul connection she had with her sister was a connection she had never felt with another human being before. The severing of it was unbearable.

She had been in contact with her brothers and her parents, and they all still seemed in disbelief and shock. Talking to her mother, she could barely form coherent sentences and sobbed most of the time they tried to talk. Her father talked crazily, somehow blaming this all on himself and his past actions.

Her eldest brother was angry at the world and himself, somehow thinking it was his job to protect Samantha from all harm. And her youngest brother, who had finally seemed less lost and more sure of himself, had become broken and reclusive. Later in the day would be the first time she would see them since they all received the news. Dread filled her. She didn't want to go.

Going back to the island facing the awful truth. Saying goodbye to Samantha would make it all absolute and final. She wanted to believe this was all a dreadful nightmare. A dream she would wake up from at any moment. Like some of the lucid dreams of her past.

They finally had everything packed and ready to go. Jessica took the picture with her. It made her feel closer to Samantha.

The mood at the Manor house was somber. Arthur helped make all the arrangements for the funeral. Betty hurriedly prepared the house and rooms for the family's arrival. Samuel made sure he plowed the driveway clear and the family cemetery was accessible.

Stella prepared comfort food that hopefully would help the family feel better. As she did, though, she broke down in tears. The thought of losing a child, even an adult child, was something a parent never wanted to endure.

She had been checking on the Zimmerman's, Zach's parents, daily and brought them meals too. Melissa was there helping her parents deal with the loss of Zach and helping to make arrangements. The Gardiners had offered to let them bury Zach in the family cemetery. They had accepted.

Stella was worried about Jimmy. He wasn't eating. The look in his eyes was reminiscent of when he had spiraled out of control before. She couldn't talk about her concerns with anyone because the family didn't know about his past. Afraid to even bring it up with Jimmy, she kept her mouth shut.

When the rest of the family got to the

Manor house around dinnertime, they hugged and cried. It was quiet. No one knew what to say. When they tried to speak, whoever it was, it would overcome them with tears.

Everyone turned in early for the night. The next day would be hard. First, they would hold the viewing in the ballroom and the memorial service. Then the caskets would go to the family cemetery by horse and carriage. Finally, they would usher mourners back to the ballroom for a late lunch after the internment.

Alone in their room, Jessica and Timothy settled in to get some sleep. Jessica couldn't hold back the tears, and as she had for every night since her sister's death, she cried herself to sleep in Timothy's arms.

Richard Jr. and Danielle were both having

a hard time dealing with the loss of Samantha and Zach. They hadn't been able to celebrate in their engagement with the overshadowing of the loss. Danielle felt guilty, feeling a bit slighted. She couldn't even be happy for herself. She also questioned whether their relationship was strong enough to withstand this hardship.

Richard Jr. had become distant the last few days. Often shunning away from her affection. When she tried to talk to him about it, he changed the subject. She wasn't trying to be unsympathetic, but if they were to be married, they would have to learn to navigate hardships together.

David withdrew since the news of his sister's death. He did his shifts, came home, ate, and then went to his room. He hadn't talked to Joe since Valentine's Day. Joe had texted and called, and David just refused to respond. Joe didn't know how to feel about being ghosted. David didn't know how to discern anything or anyone at the moment.

Losing his sister made him question life in general. Was it worth caring about anyone else? Was it worth falling in love? The pain of loss at this moment made him not want to cherish or get close to anyone ever again. He couldn't bear to feel this hurt again.

Mira and Richard hated the feeling that shrouded the Manor house. Their living children were not dealing with the loss of their sister well at all. They didn't know how to help any of them, since they struggled with their own grief.

They both felt strongly that they wanted their children to move off the island. However, they didn't know how to even bring up the subject.

Jimmy couldn't sleep. He hadn't slept in days. The fear gripped him. Something seemed off about Samantha and Zach's death. Guilt haunted him. He should have checked on them when he was leaving. Were they still alive when he left? Or were they already dead? Then the realization he had drank that night himself. There had been no beer cans, and he didn't see himself leave on the cameras. But something told him that their deaths were no accident.

Out of pure exhaustion, Jimmy fell asleep.

When he awoke to his alarm sounding, it startled him. He needed to get up and oversee the funeral preparations.

Stella was happy to see that Jimmy looked better when he came into the kitchen for some breakfast. She watched him eat, and it eased her mind a bit more that his appetite was returning.

As each family member came down and ate breakfast, the silence became deafening. A few short weeks earlier, the house had laughter and love filling it. Today, silence and sadness were filling its halls and rooms.

Jimmy went into the ballroom to ensure they set everything for the viewing. The funeral director was preparing both caskets for their loved ones to say their goodbyes. From all over, they had delivered flowers. Jimmy helped place the flowers around the coffins.

He couldn't look at Samantha or Zach lying there. At one point, he thought he saw Zach's chest rise and fall out of the corner of his eye. Then, shaking his head, he made himself look and realized it was just his imagination.

Turning around to walk out of the ballroom, Melissa standing in the doorway stopped him in his tracks. They hadn't seen each other since that night in the bar. He didn't know what to say.

Melissa didn't expect Jimmy to be helping to set up. She had just wanted to spend a few moments alone with her baby brother. But seeing Jimmy there brought back a flood of emotions. She was angry with him for what he had done the last time they saw each other. The anger bubbled up to the surface, and she couldn't hold it back.

Walking up to Jimmy, she slapped him across the face.

"I am here on the island to say goodbye to my brother only. I am not staying, and I am trying to convince my parents to leave here too. So that is my answer to your proposal."

Pushing past Jimmy to get to her brother's casket, she didn't look back. Instead, tears streamed down her face. Saying goodbye to Zach was the hardest thing she had to do, but telling the man she loved goodbye at the same time was breaking her heart into a million pieces. She had no future on the island with Jimmy, and Jimmy would never leave. So she had to let him go. The tears were both for her brother and for Jimmy.

Jimmy looked back at Melissa while rubbing his cheek. The slap hurt. Not as much as her words, though. They cut like a knife right through the center of his heart. Then, turning back to the doorway, he walked out of the room to give the woman he loved the privacy she deserved.

Melissa meant every word she spoke. She was determined for this to be the last time she stepped foot on the island. Her parents were stubborn, though. Since Zach was being buried in the Gardiner family cemetery, it would make it even harder for them to leave. She would have to give them the most heartbreaking ultimatum. Leave with her when she went, or lose her forever too. Zach was gone. Staying to be close to his grave was not a healthy decision.

Chapter 27: The Funeral

The weather didn't cooperate for the funeral, and many people could not attend who had wanted to. It was snowing pretty hard, making it impossible for the small ferry to run with the whipping winds.

A few people had got over to the island before the storm hit, and Jimmy informed Betty to make sure she prepared all spare rooms in case their guests could not leave.

Much to Jessica and Timothy's surprise, both Jack and Allison came to pay their respects. It warmed Jessica's heart to see that Jack was there for Timothy, especially since she was such a mess herself. Likewise, Allison being there was heartwarming. Considering they still hadn't figured out if there was a connection between her and Timothy. Jessica assumed she was there because she worked for the family.

Most of the mourners present were the inhabitants of the island. The Zimmerman family was sitting upfront before Zach's casket. The Gardiners sat upfront before Samantha's casket. The minister started the memorial service after everyone present paid their respects.

After his eulogy, he asked people to come up and share stories about each of the deceased's lives. Some stories brought laughter, and others brought more tears. Jessica could not get up to talk. She trembled as the sobs came forth from her body. Her brothers and parents couldn't either. It was too painful for any of them.

Melissa got up to speak of her brother.

"Thank you all for coming to pay your respects to my baby brother, Zach, and the love of his life, Samantha. I never met Samantha, but from what Zach had told me and how happy she had made him. I know she was a beautiful soul. They both were too beautiful for this world and this island. My only consolation is that they are together, and they are free from the darkness that surrounds this place."

As she finished the last sentence, she looked straight into Jimmy's eyes. The tears welled up as she sat back down with her parents. It astonished them that no one seemed shocked at her words. It was as if she spoke about what everyone had been feeling for years. The darkness that enshrouded the island was impenetrable.

The service was brief, and the procession to the cemetery was cold. Because of the cold, the mourners didn't stay long at the cemetery as the winds whipped the snow harder against the mourner's faces, freezing the tears as they fell.

They urged everyone to join them back at the ballroom for a nice warm meal, and those that could not leave could stay the night. The weather station upgraded the storm warning to a blizzard warning. Many inhabitants ate and then headed home to hunker down for the storm.

Samuel ate, and then he got to work plow-ing the roads on the island so everyone could get around. It wasn't long before the power went out. Fires were lit in all the fireplaces, and lanterns were brought out to light the rooms.

The darkness just added to the overall mood of the mourners. The Manor house got much creepier with the power being out. David first recognized one of their main security measures would be ineffective without power. It was as if he snapped out of his sadness at realizing they were all at risk. They had attributed the silence from their tormentor to the cameras. With the cameras down, that gave the harasser free rein again.

David found Jimmy and pulled him aside.

"Hey man, I know none of us want to think about what happened right before Christmas, es-

pecially right now. But, the cameras are down. No power, no cameras."

Jimmy heard him loud and clear, and it snapped him out of his funk. It was his job to make sure everyone on this island stayed safe. He already felt guilty about Samantha and Zach's deaths. He didn't want to feel any more guilt.

"Shit, David. You are right! Go up to your room. Get your drone. It's charged, right? Please tell me it's charged. Fly it out your window. Keep flying it around the perimeter of the house. We need to keep everyone here safe. We never figured out who did that crazy stuff before."

Jack and Allison had joined at a table, Jessica and Timothy. Jessica had seen David approach Jimmy and could tell by their body language something was up. She didn't want to be rude and leave Jack and Allison, so she sat there, watching her younger brother and her cousin. David left the ballroom, and Jimmy seemed to scan the room.

It was Allison who broke her focus.

"I don't know if this is a good time to discuss this."

"Discuss what?"

"Well, remember how Jack here told me how Timothy is related to him at Christmas? And his Mom took a DNA test to see if she matched with Timothy to narrow down whether it's Jack's Mom's side or Jack's dad's side."

"Yeah, we knew all that, Allison."

"The DNA came back that Jack's Mom is a

match. So Jack started asking me questions."

Both Jessica and Timothy glared at Jack. They had agreed to tread lightly with Allison and the possibility of her being related to Timothy.

Jack shrugged his shoulders.

"You two went missing in action in Ireland for a month. I couldn't wait to help solve the mystery. Sorry."

"Anyway," said Allison. "Jack asked me if I had ever been pregnant. The answer is yes. I agreed to take a DNA test too. The results came yesterday. I am a match. I am your mother, Timothy. Please forgive me for putting you up for adoption."

Timothy sat in stunned silence. Sitting

across from him was his biological mother, whom he searched for. Now that he had found her, he didn't know what to feel. Jessica was happy for Timothy. She got up and went over to hug Allison. Allison stood up and hugged her back. Then she walked over to Timothy.

"Can I hug you?"

Timothy got up and hugged his biological mother for the first time. As he felt her arms around him, he squeezed hard, and she embraced him back. Then the tears flowed, first from her and then from him. He felt unconditional love for the first time in his life. Allison never thought this day would happen. She had never wanted to know the child she gave up for adoption. Now knowing him, hugging him for the first time, she never wanted to let him go.

As Jessica watched mother and son, they let go and sat back down to get acquainted with one another. She was happy for them both. However, part of her couldn't help but feel a bit of worry after what she had just endured. Finding her biological family, bonding with her sister, and then losing her sister in a matter of months. She didn't want Timothy to experience that. She prayed their reunion would stay happy.

Allison told them she was 15 when she had become pregnant. She didn't go into detail. However, she said that the pregnancy was a product of rape. This was a gut punch to Timothy, and Jessica could see it on his face. She reached over and squeezed his hand.

Allison explained that even though he

was a product of rape, she could not fathom aborting him. To her, it felt as if that would punish him for something he didn't do wrong. So she just prayed the whole time he would be more like her.

She explained how she wound up in a psych ward for the duration of her pregnancy. First, her parents didn't believe her claims of rape, especially when she refused to get an abortion. Then she wound up being committed when she had a full-fledged breakdown.

This wound up being a blessing for her because she could carry him to term and make all the preparations to have him adopted. In addition, it saved her parents the embarrassment of their daughter's pregnancy. Although they weren't too embarrassed to tell their friends, their daughter was in a psych ward.

After giving birth and being released from the psychiatric hospital, she couldn't wait to turn sixteen and pursue emancipation from her parents. Their lack of support of her through the most challenging time in her life had opened her eyes to the toxic relationship she had with them. This had been a driving factor for her to give up her child for adoption. She felt she didn't know how to be a good parent.

Timothy's heart broke for his biological mother hearing her retell her story. However, he felt she was brave, and he appreciated everything she had gone through to give him life.

Upstairs, David had gotten his drone out. He opened the window to his bedroom, facing the front circular driveway. The snow was still coming down at a blinding pace, and the wind was whipping. He didn't know if the drone would fly in this weather. He was determined to try, though. Controlling the drone proved difficult. He made one complete pass around the house.

As he was going for the second pass, he heard Samuel's plow truck coming up the front driveway. It stopped in front of the house, just under the open window. Samuel left the truck running and carried a thermos into the house.

Within minutes, David heard someone enter his room. By the time he reacted and turned around, feeling himself being shoved out the second-story window. The blizzard raging outside muffled his yell for help.

When Samuel returned to his truck, the

gruesome scene met him. It seemed David had fallen out of his window onto the snowplow blade. Samuel ran into the ballroom to get help.

By the time he reached Jimmy, told him what he had found, and had returned to David, he had bled to death. Jimmy was in shock at what he saw. He contacted the coast guard to have David's body removed from the island since they could not run the ferry during the storm. He accompanied the body to the main-land. Richard Jr. had been put in charge of in-vestigating the accident.

Richard Jr. taped off David's room and didn't allow anyone in or out. He wanted to make sure everything was how they found it when the police came. So, setting up guards in-side and outside the house, he made sure nothing was touched.

This annoyed Samuel because he couldn't use his truck to plow, and he had to resort to the backhoe to keep the roads on the island clear.

Everyone was in shock. Especially Mira and Richard. They had just buried their youngest daughter, and now they had lost their youngest son to a tragic accident. Richard made Mira a potent drink and brought her to their room to rest. He was worried she was about to have a breakdown.

Jessica and Timothy couldn't fathom what had occurred. They had been so busy getting to know Allison and her story that they hadn't seen or heard anything out of the ordinary until Samuel came in to get Jimmy.

Jessica's stomach lurched, and she told Timothy she needed to go to their room. They showed Allison and Jack to their rooms for the night and then went to theirs. Jessica made it into the bathroom before her stomach let loose.

Mourning her sister's death, her sister's boyfriend's death, and now the death of her youngest brother was too much for her. She had always felt she was a sound person, but this, this was too much for one person to handle.

Timothy didn't know what to say or do. His emotions were on a rollercoaster. He was happy that he had found his biological mother. Still, it was devastating with the loss of Samantha, Zach, and now David.

That feeling of dread crept back over both of them. It was as if Timothy and Jessica both knew in the pit of their stomachs it was no coincidence that Samantha and Zach overdosed and David fell to his death.

Both of their minds wandered back to the night of Alexandria's fall. She had been pushed. Even though the police closed the case because of Mary's suicide note confession, they still did not know who. They now knew they were dealing with a serial killer targeting their family.

Sleep eluded most of the occupants of the Manor house that evening. The events had made it hard for anyone to feel safe, and the blizzard raging outside didn't help.

In the morning, the blizzard had stopped. It had dumped two feet of snow on the island. Jimmy returned with the state police, and they began their investigation. They questioned everyone that had been present.

The police went over David's room with a fine-tooth comb. There was no evidence of foul play found. Ruling his death an accident, they left the family to deal with their grief.

Chapter 28: Unexpected Opportunity

They had gotten rid of another one. Their power was growing with each kill. They loved how opportunities just dropped in their laps. It was becoming easier and easier.

The storm had provided a perfect opportunity for them to size up the family and possibly take out another member.

With the power being out, they knew the cameras would be ineffective. Also, the storm gave them plenty of work to do and a plausible alibi. They just needed to be observant and find the perfect opportunity.

It didn't take long for the opportunity to

arise.

They saw the youngest Gardiner boy next to his open second-story window as they worked. They seized on the opportunity and pushed him out the window. He couldn't have landed more perfectly on the snowplow blade.

No one seemed to suspect them. Even the police in the morning had found no evidence of foul play and ruled it a tragic accident.

They loved when a plan fell into place.

Witnessing the unraveling of the family was sweet revenge. They wanted them all to suffer. To feel misery. They had overheard Richard speaking with Mira.

His guilt over the deaths of his cousins was coming back to haunt him.

Mira was on the verge of a mental break-down, setting up for possibilities of her demise.

Jimmy, not eating or sleeping, was also playing right into everything.

They needed to keep the family close, though. They needed to prolong their misery.

The only way they could accomplish that was to make sure the family needed to stay on the island.

Now to make sure that goal came to fruition.

Plans needed to be made.

They couldn't be found out.

Chapter 29: Love and Loss

The police finished interviewing Allison and Jack, and they headed off the island and back to the city. As much as they felt for the family and their grief, it thoroughly freaked them out. Melissa's words echoed in their minds, and the eerie silence of the inhabitants after she spoke the words made David's tragic death almost prophetic. It had been a whirlwind of a night between the blizzard and David's death.

Timothy was sad to see his family leave in one respect, and in another, he wanted them off the island, where they could be safe. However, their goodbyes were short, and they promised to stay in touch.

Jessica just wanted to crawl back into her bed. She tried to cover up with the blankets and disappear into the dream world where her sister and brother were still happily alive. Where Samantha visited her, and they shared secrets again. Where David was happy and free. But sleep was eluding her. Making her face the grim reality of her life. When she joined the others in the dining room, she sensed a shift in their world.

There was tension between Danielle and Richard Jr. It was so thick. Their body language showed a divide in their relationship. Danielle sat at the dining room table with her arms folded, deep in thought. Richard Jr. was in a serious discussion across the room with

Jimmy about upping security measures, his back to Danielle. They seemed as if they were in two separate worlds.

Jessica observed and felt sad for them both. She wondered what was going on with them and whether they could patch things up. Then, abruptly, Danielle got up from the table and left the room. Richard Jr. didn't even seem to notice. However, he noticed when she returned with two suitcases. Looking at her, confused.

"What are those for?"

"I am going home. I need space from this place. And from you, from us. I will be here for David's funeral, but I can't stay here anymore. This place is filled with evil. Melissa was right."

Finishing her statement, she took the engagement ring off her finger. She handed it to Richard Jr. She kissed him on the cheek, with tears streaming down her face, and walked out the door to her car.

Richard Jr. Stood there in complete shock. His worst fear had just materialized before his eyes. It splintered the rest of his heart into a thousand pieces.

Part of him wanted to run after Danielle and beg her to stay, and the other part of him said even though he was hurting, this was the best thing for both of them. This way, he knew she would be safe forever.

Jessica watched in awe. *Was that a ring she just handed back? When did that happen?* She was confused and heartbroken for her brother.

Jimmy put his hand on Richard Jr.'s shoulder.

"Sorry, man. I know that has to hurt."

"She's gotta do what she's gotta do. And I gotta do what I gotta do. Right now, my focus is catching this psychopath who is killing our family. We all know deep down this was no accident. And we all know deep down that Samantha and Zach didn't overdose. So, how are we going to stop this person from killing us all off?"

Richard Jr. finally verbalized what they were all feeling. He was right. They all knew it. Danielle knew it. She was the smart one. She left.

At that moment, Jessica craved the solitude of her previous life. She may have felt lonely, but at least she was safe. Then she felt guilty for even thinking that. Jessica loved

Timothy and her biological family. With love came risk. She knew that. She just never thought it would be her life at risk.

Adding to Jimmy's stress with upping security measures, Matt Zimmerman had notified him he was retiring and moving off the island. Losing Zach was too much for them. He and his wife were moving to upstate New York to be closer to their only living child, Melissa. That meant security was missing three men, leaving them even more short-staffed.

They spent the next couple of days preparing for David's funeral. It seemed like Déjà vu for them all. They were tired and weary of all the loss.

Mira and Richard stayed up in their room except for meals. Mira had spiraled into a deep depression, and Richard was desperately try-ing to help her through it. The guilt he was feeling about everything that had happened to his family increased every day. He fully be-lieved all that was occurring was karma for the sins he had committed in his life.

Contemplating ending it all, he thought maybe Mary had the right idea. Perhaps he could release his karma and spare his family any more heartache. But then Richard knew Mira could not live without him. Losing him would end her beautiful life, and he could not do that to her. He could not put his children through any more loss, either.

The Zimmerman's said their goodbyes to the Gardiners the day before David's funeral. They had apologized, they would not be there to attend. They explained they just couldn't handle another funeral of someone so young. The Gardiners understood.

Before they left, Melissa found Jimmy alone.

"I am sorry for slapping you the other day. I was angry and hurt. But I meant every word I said. I will not be back, ever. I convinced my parents to leave. So now I have no reason to come back. I love you, Jimmy, I always have, But I can't live here. So if you ever leave, look me up."

Melissa gave Jimmy a quick kiss on the cheek.

"I can't leave. My family is here. I love you, Melissa. I always have and always will, but this is my home. Like it or not."

"Take your mother and father with you, Jimmy. Save yourself and them from the evil that surrounds this place."

"They aren't my only family here."

As he let the words tumble out of his mouth. The secret that he had kept for months, he turned and walked away from the love of his life. He didn't want her to see the tears forming in his eyes.

The realization that he had an obligation to the Gardiner family, to his family, weighed heavily on his shoulders. He wished he could take his adoptive parents and run, but he couldn't.

Instead, he had to face the evil and try to bring it to justice. Maybe if he did, Melissa could return, and they could have their happily ever after.

Melissa stood there, stunned. She didn't understand the words he had spoken. Not at first. Later, she thought about his sudden move to the Manor house after the deaths of Alexandria and Mary. Then it clicked. He had to be some long-lost Gardiner relative.

The wheels in her mind turned. The stories about Mary Gardiner's child that she had lost. They explored every inch of Gardiners Island as kids, including the family cemetery. They had seen the infant's grave. But, there were warnings not to bring it up to Ms. Mary, ever.

Zach had told her all about Samantha's sister, Jessica, and the scandal surrounding her birth and adoption. But he didn't tell her

Jimmy was also a Gardiner. Wouldn't Zach have known? Maybe he didn't. Maybe there was a reason they kept his secret. Could Jimmy be that child?

Melissa's thoughts went to the deer carcasses that Zach had told her about. Whoever was killing those deer was clearly a psychopath. She had done enough studying of psychology to know that. It hit her like a ton of bricks. She needed answers from Jimmy. When she got home, she would sit down and write him a letter. The drive home was torturous.

David's funeral was small, with mostly family. At least this time, the weather was sunny, even with the snow-covered ground. Joe showed up, and when everyone else had headed back to the ballroom for the luncheon, he quietly placed a bouquet of white roses on David's casket.

Jessica was the only one who witnessed this act of love. As she did, tears streamed down her face. Then she approached Joe and hugged him.

"Thank you for loving my brother when he didn't know how to love himself."

About The Author

D. M. Foley

A former paraeducator, novice genealogist, turned author, D.M. Foley is an award-winning writer. Her first book, The Lyons Garden Book One Family Ties, received The New York Best Sellers Gold Award in December 2021. She lives in Southeastern, Ct. with her husband of 27 years and her three sons.

You can follow her on her social media accounts at:
D.M. Foley - Author Page on Facebook
@d.m._foley on Instagram and TikTok
and
@DMFoley on Twitter

Contact information:
d.m.foleyauthor@gmail.com

Books In This Series

The Lyons Garden

Family Ties Book One

Erasing Secrets Book Two

Books By This Author

The Lyons Garden Book One Family Ties

Made in United States
North Haven, CT
05 March 2022

16790462R00275